RISING ABOVE

GENEVIEVE FORTIN

BELLA
BOOKS
2019

Bella Books, Inc.
P.O. Box 10543
Tallahassee, FL 32302

Printed in the United States of America on acid-free paper.

First Bella Books Edition 2019

Editor: Ann Roberts
Cover Designer: Judith Fellows

ISBN: 978-1-64247-020-8

Other Bella Books by Genevieve Fortin

Dingo's Recovery
First Fall
Two Kinds of Elizabeth
Water's Edge

Acknowledgments

Some novels start with a character or a location. This novel was built around a conflict: a scientist who believes the best way to deal with rising sea levels is to relocate away from coastlines, and an innkeeper who can't imagine living anywhere else. I can't remember how exactly that idea came to mind but I am grateful it did because it changed my life. I've always believed in climate change, of course, and I've always been concerned. The research I did to write this novel, however, brought me to a new level of awareness I might not have reached without it. It changed the way I plan to live my life moving forward. That said, *Rising Above* is about love before anything else. Love between two women, but also love for the sea.

I'd like to thank Linda, Jessica, and the entire Bella Books team for letting me tell the stories I want to tell. My editor Ann Roberts, who helped me dig deeper into Ana's character and make this book so much better. I feel fortunate I had the privilege to learn from an author I admire. Denise who, like Melodie, might have saltwater running through her veins. I wouldn't be surprised. Loving her brings me closer to the sea and I am grateful for that. And as always, I'd like to thank every reader who picked this book or any of my books. They wouldn't be the same without you.

About the Author

Genevieve is French Canadian but claims her heart holds dual citizenship. Not surprising since she lived in the USA for thirteen years and still visits every chance she gets. Besides writing and reading, her passions include traveling, decadent desserts, fruity martinis, and watching HGTV. For now she lives in St-Georges, just a few miles north of the border between Maine and Quebec. She and her partner share a house with their two dogs, Spike and Betty.

Dedication

To all of us who love the sea and understand
she needs *her* space…

CHAPTER ONE

Present

Ana enjoyed the sound of the hard snow crunching under her winter boots as she walked closer to the Saint-Laurent River. It had to be this cold for the snow to make that sound. Cold enough for her nostrils to stick together and for her breath to hang in the air like a fog. She took her gloves off, placed them in her jacket pockets, and reached for her camera in her backpack. She simply had to take a few shots of the scene before her. Snow and ice rippled over the sea, as if the waves had frozen into place. The white of the snow met with a brighter, thin white horizon before it faded into a light gray tinted sky.

The monochrome December panorama was breathtaking—quite literally. She took a deep breath that burned her lungs. She immortalized the view with a few simple clicks and then shot a brief video, wanting to capture the sound of the wind, but mostly the silence of the sea. That silence was almost troubling. No waves soothing her mind with their regular rhythm or crashing on the large, flat rocks that covered part of the beach. This place and moment gave her a new understanding of an expression she'd never stopped to think about before: the dead of the winter. It made more sense now as she looked around her. The perfect, peaceful dead of winter.

Ana's bare hands were so cold that it felt like tiny needles pushing into her fingertips. The good news was that the great tides expected in the next few days wouldn't cause damage, she reasoned as she blew warm air into her cupped hands. At twenty-five below zero degrees Fahrenheit, she could hear deniers snicker in her mind. *So much for global warming, huh, fancy scientist?* Damn deniers. Their refusal to acknowledge the difference between weather events and long-term climate trends was mind-blowing. And dangerous. Idiots, she thought as she dismissively shook her head. She wouldn't let her mind clutter with her usual preoccupations. Not now. Not when she'd finally made her way back to Sainte-Luce-Sur-Mer.

She turned around and took a picture of the small hotel she was so happy to see again before she placed the camera safely in her backpack and put her gloves back on. She stared at the charming inn, its white walls, wraparound porch and its mansard flared roof. She was glad they'd been able to repaint the exterior as planned. She hesitated before she walked toward the front of the property where she'd parked her electric car. She grabbed her luggage out of the trunk, took another deep breath, and rolled her suitcase toward the hotel. She paused at the bottom of the stairs and smiled at the large wooden sign bearing the logo of the hotel: an illustrated sheep running on water with the words *Auberge du Mouton Blanc* forming a half circle over its head. The White Sheep Inn. The place where she wanted to be more than anywhere else in the world. And the place she most feared entering at the same time.

She recognized the annoying bell announcing her arrival. When she opened the door, she immediately saw her. Melodie. Standing behind the reception desk with her back to her, she was using the counter that lined up the wall to fold towels. "*Une minute,*" she said in French without turning around.

Ana took off her gloves and let go of her luggage when she saw Miller run to her. She crouched down to pet the Cardigan

Welsh Corgi. He'd gained some weight. She'd never doubted the dog would recognize her and would be happy to see her again. She'd been right, judging by his wagging tail and wet tongue on her hand. Miller was the easy part of this reunion.

She straightened up and smiled at Thomas, who stood proudly in a small playpen behind the reception desk. Her heart clenched at the sight of the toddler. He'd grown so much. He could stand on his own now. He could probably walk, she imagined, which explained the playpen filled with toys that kept him from wandering. His dark hair was even thicker than it had been, but it was just as unruly. His eyes had remained blue, almost as light as his mother's. He waved at her and laughed a loud, beautiful, contagious laugh. She felt her smile widen even as she fought tears. She'd missed so much. Too much. She waved back at him, wondering if he'd recognized her or if he was this friendly with all strangers. Ana had not realized she'd moved closer as she'd focused on Thomas, but she was practically leaning over the reception desk when Melodie finally turned around and saw her.

In the mere few seconds that followed, Ana saw three distinct expressions on Melodie's face. The first was pure shock as her Arctic blue eyes opened wide and she gasped. The second was so brief Ana wasn't sure she hadn't imagined it, but she thought she'd seen a moment of joy, or at least relief, pass through soft eyes and a twitch of her full lips that resembled a smile. The third expression was the easiest to recognize. It settled in Melodie's clenched teeth and the way she squinted at her before she spoke with undisguised anger. "Anais Bloom. What the hell are you doing here?"

CHAPTER TWO

One year earlier

"Please be quiet," Melodie Beaulieu whispered to her six-month-old son as she paced behind the reception desk, lightly bouncing him up and down and patting his bottom. Nothing worked. His diaper was dry, she'd fed him, and she'd been holding him for half an hour. Thomas should have been perfectly content, but he was still screaming to the top of his tiny lungs. The dark wood planks of the floor squeaked under each of her steps, accompanying her son's cries.

The young couple checking out of the inn kept glancing at her, although she was doing all she could to disappear against the back wall while her grandmother, Yvonne, handled the customers. She tried to focus on the floral pattern of the wallpaper behind the couple to avoid their scrutiny but wasn't successful. She smiled and mouthed the word "sorry." The woman smiled at her sympathetically, but the man cringed when Thomas hit a particularly high note. He even shook his head when he finally grabbed their luggage and left the lobby.

"I'm so sorry," Melodie said to her grandmother, who was already taking Thomas out of her arms.

"Let me try."

Thomas almost instantly stopped crying when Yvonne did the exact same reassuring bouncing and patting she'd been doing to no avail. She wanted to cry with frustration but took a deep breath instead. Thomas closed his eyes.

"Now why wouldn't he do this for me?"

"Because you're way too anxious, dear. You panicked and managed to stress out everyone around you, but most of all this little angel," she explained as she lay him in the small bassinet they'd placed behind the reception desk. Melodie had to admit Yvonne was right about her anxiety level. She freaked out every time Thomas made any noise in the presence of customers. She couldn't help but smile at her grandmother's contrasting calm and assurance.

Yvonne had always been her role model—strong, independent, business savvy, but also tender and caring. At seventy-four, Yvonne didn't look a day over fifty, and the only reason why she was finally talking about retirement was that she'd recently been diagnosed with Parkinson's disease.

That information had not registered in Melodie's brain yet. Yvonne stood tall and straight, with her perfectly shaped, short blond bob and her piercing blue eyes. If Melodie hadn't witnessed an occasional tremor in her right hand, she wouldn't believe her grandmother was sick.

"I told you I didn't mind keeping Thomas with us for now because it's slow, but you do realize you'll have to figure out something before business picks up, right?"

Yvonne usually closed the White Sheep Inn during winter, as did most establishments in Sainte-Luce-Sur-Mer. It didn't make sense to keep hotels open in the cold months when tourists deserted their little beach community. This winter, however, she'd decided the off-season would be the perfect opportunity to teach Melodie how to manage the small family business. Since they'd started Melodie's training in November, they'd never had more than two of their eight available rooms occupied at a time. A month later Melodie was getting used to the daily tasks of an innkeeper, but she still couldn't imagine handling them with a full house. She was grateful her grandmother had decided to entrust her with the White Sheep Inn, but she was terrified she'd fail the woman she most loved and respected. The anxiety that had temporarily loosened its grip on her when Thomas had fallen asleep was back in full force. "I know, Mammie. I simply can't afford daycare right now."

Melodie and Thomas were staying in the hotel during her training. The off-season was a good time to learn how to manage a hotel, but by definition it was not a lucrative period. Yvonne had graciously offered to lodge and feed them so Melodie could quit her job as a server at Normandin's Restaurant and focus on her new career as an innkeeper, but she couldn't ask her grandmother to pay for daycare as well.

"What about Kevin? Can't he help?"

Melodie scoffed. "All Kevin cares about are his dirt bikes and drinking beer with his buds. You know that. Besides, he's going back out west after the holidays."

Yvonne sighed heavily and folded towels that sat in a laundry basket under the desk. Melodie hurried to help her. She should have folded them earlier. When would she start anticipating every task instead of simply following her grandmother's lead? Yvonne hadn't said another word, but her movements were more abrupt than usual and Melodie could feel her exasperation.

"Please say what's on your mind." When Yvonne didn't reply, Melodie continued. "Okay then, I'll do it for you. Didn't I know Kevin was a selfish prick before I slept with him? Yes, I did. I don't know what I saw in him or why I did what I did, but it's done. I have Thomas now. Do you really think I planned on raising a baby as a single mother at thirty?" She folded the towels with the same energy as Yvonne, both women beating them into submission. Yvonne folded the last one before she turned to Melodie and took that calm but assertive tone that made Melodie feel like a little child.

"No, that's not what I think at all. I don't think you've ever planned anything in your life, dear. If you really want to know what I was thinking, there you have it. And I was also wondering if I shouldn't have let you move to Montreal with Nicole instead of helping your dad raise you. I love my son to death, but we both know he wasn't what you needed at that age."

Melodie was fourteen when her parents divorced, and her mother moved to Montreal to focus on a career in marketing. She felt her eyes fill with tears. Her grandmother knew better than to bring up her mother in a conversation. In any conversation. She finally found the nerve to answer, but her voice was barely audible when she did. "Where is this coming from? You know I wanted to stay here with dad."

"I know, but you were too young to know what was best for you." Yvonne took a deep breath that seemed to calm her. She took Melodie's hands and when she spoke again, her tone was much softer. "You know I love Thomas, right?" She nodded. "I'm not saying I'm not happy we have him. Far from it. But I can't help wondering lately if Montreal might have been a better place for you. It's a big city. Perhaps you could have met someone special."

Melodie squeezed her grandmother's hands as she finally understood what this outburst was really about. "A woman? You think it would have been easier for me to meet a nice woman and fall in love if I'd lived in Montreal?"

"Well, don't you?"

"Maybe. But I would've been miserable. You know that, Mammie. My place is here, by the sea. And there are lesbians around here, you know." Melodie laughed and was relieved when Yvonne joined in. "I just suck at picking them. Men, women, it doesn't matter. I'm no good at love. And it's not because I didn't have good role models. I had the best. You and Pappy. You always looked so happy."

"We were," Yvonne confirmed as she glanced at the black and white wedding portrait hung on the back wall of the lobby. Melodie followed her grandmother's gaze. She'd always loved that portrait. As a young girl she'd been fascinated with the oval golden frame and its ornate ruffled edge, but the comforting smiles of her grandparents and the undeniable love between them were what she loved most about it. Raymond Beaulieu had died of a heart attack five years earlier, but they'd been happily married and in love for close to fifty years.

"Now, please do not ever think you should have sent me to Montreal with my mother. I know I give you lots of reasons to worry about me. I'm sorry about that, but there is only one thing I'm one hundred percent sure about in my life and that one thing is that my place is here. With you, with dad, and now with Thomas. No matter what stupid choice I make in the future, I will never, ever doubt that my place is here and I don't want you to doubt it either. Okay?"

"Okay, if you say so." Yvonne offered an understanding smile before she added, "And we'll figure out something about daycare. Together."

"Thank you." She hugged her tightly before she took the laundry basket full of clean, folded towels from her grandmother and headed toward the wooden staircase that led to the guest rooms. She didn't want Yvonne to see the tears in her eyes as she remembered that her mother had not actually asked her to move to Montreal with her after the divorce. She would have said no, as she'd always told her dad and grandmother she had. Her place was in Sainte-Luce-Sur-Mer. That much was true. But they would never know that the option to leave had never even been on the table for her to consider.

CHAPTER THREE

Ana got out of her car and stretched as she would after a long night of sleep. She joined her hands over her head and reached as high as she could before she lightly bent at the waist, one side and then the other. She'd only stopped twice during her six-hundred and sixty mile journey from Ithaca to Sainte-Luce-Sur-Mer, and although her Chevy Bolt was comfortable, she knew she'd pay the price for sitting so long. Her lower back hurt and her legs were numb. She walked the length of the parking lot to slowly wake her aching body and take in the seascape that extended behind the small hotel. The strong winds created foam crested waves on the Saint-Laurent River, and she had to admit she could see why some people compared them to a herd of white sheep running on water. It was a little too poetic for her scientific taste, but she could see it. She might as well, since she was going to stay in a place called the White Sheep Inn for the next few weeks.

She'd never been to Sainte-Luce-Sur-Mer but she knew the thirty-seven degrees Fahrenheit temperature she'd noted on her car display screen was much warmer than usual December temperatures in this region of Quebec. The river was not frozen and the locals were probably worried about the potential great tides the upcoming winter solstice might bring. If low atmospheric pressure and strong winds got into the mix, they could witness a storm surge comparable to the one they'd lived through in December of 2010. Or worse. The storm had caused millions of dollars in damages, and in this small beach community alone, forty-six homes had been judged beyond repair and had to be demolished. Perhaps their fear that history might repeat itself would make it easier to convince them to participate in her interviews. She hoped so.

She took a deep breath and filled her lungs with sea air. She couldn't help but smile as she realized she hadn't breathed this deeply in months. Hadn't felt this free. She'd left Ithaca the day after her mother's funeral. In August, the doctors had told Constance that nothing could be done for her widely spread metastatic cancer besides keeping her relatively comfortable with pain medication. Ana had decided to take a sabbatical from her position as Associate Professor in the Earth and Atmospheric Sciences program of Cornell University and invited her mother to live with her in her small two-bedroom home. It was the right thing to do.

She did it out of obligation more than love. She hated to admit it even to herself, but like the forty-six homes that had been destroyed on this beach in 2010, her relationship with her mother had already been beyond repair at that point. She did what Constance wanted her to do until the end, indulged her every whim. Unlike the little girl who'd hoped for love and affection in return, however, she'd learned not to expect anything but selfishness and criticism from the woman.

In the four months leading to her mother's death, they'd emptied and sold Constance's small condo and put her affairs in order. There was nothing pressing to do after the services, nothing to keep her in Ithaca. She needed to leave.

The news she'd received a few weeks before her mother's death had only confirmed her need to come to Sainte-Luce-

Sur-Mer. She was told she would not get the grant to study the effects of climate changes and the rise of sea levels on the coastal life of the Bas-Saint-Laurent region. She'd been encouraged to redirect her research to larger and better known coastal communities such as Miami or New York City, but she'd argued that those large cities were already getting enough attention. She was much more intrigued with a small community where the government had ruled people would no longer be allowed to build less than a hundred feet from the river and where there seemed to be a will to help people relocate farther from the rising water. That mentality was much more in line with her own than projects to build a wall to protect New York City from the ocean or to raise Miami above sea level one street at a time.

She realized those large-scale projects should have excited her as an engineering geologist, but it was no longer the case. So she figured she would take the rest of her sabbatical year to conduct her own research anyway. The money her mother had left her from the sale of her condo would help. She couldn't explain exactly why, but she needed this research and she needed to be here.

She entered the lobby of the inn and cringed at the loud sound of the bell. She was immediately taken aback by how old the hotel actually looked. She'd read it had been built in the late 1890s when she'd made her reservation online, but she'd assumed it had been somewhat modernized over the years. The textured roses on the wallpaper, the wide planks of the floors, the ornate crown moulding, and the dark wood of the reception desk all seemed original. Others might have found the decor charming, but to Ana, it was stifling and oppressive. She hoped the guest rooms at least had been updated.

She moved closer to the desk and noticed an empty bassinet and a dog sleeping on the ground. The dog opened one eye to look at her and went back to sleep with a heavy sigh. She could hear a baby crying from somewhere in the building, perhaps upstairs. What kind of hotel was this? Fortunately the lady on the other side of the desk looked professional when she smiled and greeted her in French. *"Bonjour. Bienvenue à l'Auberge du Mouton Blanc."*

"Sorry, I don't speak French. But I have a reservation for Anais Bloom."

"Oh yes, of course. Anais. What a lovely name," the woman replied with a heavy accent.

"Thank you. I don't really like it, though. I go by Ana."

"I see. Ana it is, then. I have a room with a view of the Saint-Laurent for you. It's our best room."

"Great," Ana answered before a younger woman rushed into the lobby and went straight behind the reception desk holding a crying baby in her arms and addressing the older woman in French. She seemed furious and spoke as if Ana didn't exist. Ana didn't understand French but recognized the name Kevin in the middle of the woman's rant. She figured the women were related, judging by the ice blue eyes they shared. Ana had never seen eyes that light before, almost white.

The younger woman could have been attractive. She had lovely curves, thick light brown curls falling below her shoulders, and dimples punctuating a beautiful round face. But she was beyond rude. Ana hoped she didn't work at the hotel because she was obviously clueless when it came to customer service. And would someone make that baby stop screaming already? Her ears couldn't take it much longer. More importantly, one of his basic needs was obviously not being met. She had a feeling that need was the same peace and quiet she needed right now. She hoped that rude woman would calm down quickly for his benefit even more than hers. She was tempted to turn around and leave, but she knew she'd have to go to Rimouski to find another hotel that was open in winter, and she wanted to be in Sainte-Luce-Sur-Mer, right by the Saint-Laurent.

The women continued talking in French as the older of the two took the baby and he finally stopped crying. "I'm very sorry about this interruption, Ana. We have a little emergency as you can see. Melodie here will show you to your room if you don't mind."

"Sure," Ana agreed reluctantly.

Melodie took a key from a series of hooks behind the desk without acknowledging Ana's presence and didn't bother to smile when she turned and commanded, "Follow me."

Ana didn't expect Melodie to carry her luggage upstairs for her, but she could have offered. She could certainly have slowed down instead of hurrying upstairs and waiting for her with an air of exasperation as she fidgeted with the key. It was an actual key, not a card, which left Ana much less hopeful regarding any possible renovation that might have been done in the guest rooms. "Yours is right there," Melodie announced without enthusiasm as she pointed to the first door on the left and handed Ana the red plastic circular key chain with a faded, black number one.

"Thanks," Ana said more automatically than graciously.

"Breakfast is served every morning between seven and nine. The dining room is on the left at the bottom of the stairs. Enjoy your stay," Melodie said in one breath before she ran back downstairs without giving Ana the opportunity to ask a question.

"I guess she works here after all," she muttered to herself as she struggled with the lock on the door. When she finally entered the room, she had to laugh to keep from crying, completely deflated. The floral pattern of the wallpaper was orange instead of pink, and the wide boards of the floor were a lighter shade of wood, but, like the lobby, there was no doubt the decor was original and so depressively old.

The floor squeaked as she rolled her suitcase into the room and hurried to the bathroom, almost expecting to find a porcelain chamber pot in which she would be expected to urinate. There was one, but fortunately there was also a flush toilet. The chamber pot was simply a decorative element sitting on the antique wood dresser that had been converted into a bathroom vanity. The shower-bath combo was small, but she turned the water tap to the left and was satisfied when she felt warm water on her hand. She would have preferred a more modern look, but she had to admit this fitted better with the rest of the place.

She stepped back into the small room and noticed another antique dresser by the bed and an antique armoire on the opposite wall. She cringed when she spotted the crucifix above the bed. Really? How was that still allowed in this day and age?

She shrugged and figured that if the mattress was comfortable enough, she could sleep with Jesus above her head for a while. The bed was also from the Victorian era, made of white-painted wood with a curved headboard. She sat carefully on the mattress and was relieved to find it was not too soft or too firm. She bounced on it a few times and the bed squeaked with each movement. "Oh hell."

CHAPTER FOUR

"I can't believe he's doing this to me again," Melodie continued as soon as she returned to the reception desk. "He begged to have Thomas this weekend, and when I finally give in and make plans of my own, he cancels everything." She was boiling with anger. The next time Kevin Cloutier remembered he had a son and asked to take him for a weekend, she'd tell him to go to hell.

"What I don't understand is why you're so surprised," her grandmother said as she dusted the reception desk with an old-fashioned feather duster.

Melodie grabbed the glass cleaner and paper towels under the desk and worked on the windows, channelling some of her anger through stronger-and-faster-than-needed scrubbing and wiping. "I'm not surprised. I'm pissed off. Sophie's in town tonight but she's going back to Quebec tomorrow morning. We'd planned to have a few drinks and catch up. I haven't seen her in over a year. I haven't gone out with any of my friends in over a month, Mammie. He knows that, but of course he doesn't give a shit."

"Sophie Berger? From high school?"

"I don't know any other Sophie," she hissed with an irritated click of the tongue.

"Whoa. Do you hear the way you're talking to me? You need to calm down right now and change your tone or I won't help you, is that clear?"

Melodie stopped rubbing the window and leaned her forehead against her arm, the cold of the window pane reaching her face and cooling her down. She'd always had quite a temper. No, she'd always been impulsive, but her fits of temper had started when she was a teenager. Her grandmother had even brought her to a counsellor to work on anger management skills. He'd given her great tips, but she'd refused to see him again after he'd suggested a session with her mother. Nicole was in Montreal and Melodie wouldn't ask her to come back for a therapy session with her fourteen-year-old daughter. She probably wouldn't come anyway. Besides, it didn't take a genius to figure out Melodie's anger had something to do with her departure. She'd used his tips and had learned to better control her choleric impulses on her own over the years, but sometimes she still lost it.

Kevin was particularly good at triggering her anger, and unfortunately he was a trigger she couldn't avoid if she wanted her son to know his father, which she did. She hated these outbursts, especially when she was disrespectful to her grandmother. She took a deep breath and turned to Yvonne. "You're right. I'm sorry. I didn't mean to talk to you that way."

"But you did. When all you had to do was come to me and explain you needed someone to take care of Thomas while you went out with Sophie. When have I ever refused to take care of him?"

Melodie felt her lips twitch into a smile as her grandmother spoke. "I know. I should have known better. Thank you so much for doing this for me. And again I'm so sorry about being rude to you." She hugged her grandmother and turned to leave so she could get ready for her night out.

"Not so quick," Yvonne called behind her. She turned and realized her grandmother's reprimanding stance had not disappeared yet. Her lips pinched and she narrowed her eyes.

"What? I really didn't mean to talk to you that way, Mammie. I'm really sorry."

"I know, but I'm not the only one you need to apologize to," Yvonne explained as she rolled her eyes and jerked her head upward to indicate the second floor where Melodie had left their only guest for the night. She hadn't noticed much about the American woman except for pale skin and expensive designer winter clothes. She was tall, at least three inches taller than her own five feet six. Her thick, short auburn hair was tousled and clashed with her overall appearance of rich tourist with a stick up her butt. Melodie wondered now what she could be doing here in the middle of winter. She hadn't cared earlier.

"That woman? Why would I apologize to her?"

"Do you really think the way you welcomed her is appropriate? You were impolite and you embarrassed me." Melodie lowered her gaze to the floor, ashamed. Embarrassing her grandmother was the worst sensation she'd ever known, one she'd always desperately tried to avoid, but one she'd been faced with multiple times nonetheless. Yvonne moved closer to her and spoke softly. "You have to better understand customer service if you want to survive in this business. If you act that way in the summer when customers have other options, they will take their business somewhere else."

"I understand, but she arrived at the wrong moment."

"No. Don't even try. The only bad moment for a customer to arrive is when we're closed." Melodie nodded sheepishly. "Customers don't care about your problems. And they shouldn't have to. They come here for a comfortable room, a good meal, and a great experience. They don't come here to be subjected to your personal struggles or emotions." Yvonne patted Melodie's hand and smiled. "Do you understand how important this is? It's probably the most essential part of this business. Customers who come back every year don't come only for the view and the charm of the place. They come back for us, too."

"Okay, I get it, but do I really need to apologize to her? What if I promise I'll be extra nice for the remainder of her stay?"

Yvonne patted her hand one last time and went back to her dusting before she spoke again. "You will apologize. Over breakfast tomorrow. Now go have fun with Sophie. And say hi for me." Melodie knew there was no point arguing with that tone. She'd think of something to say to the American. But for now she looked forward to a relaxing night out with her best friend.

CHAPTER FIVE

Melodie installed Thomas in the stroller and chuckled, which made him smile in return. His smile was so precious. She couldn't help but laugh at the way he lay there in his snow pouch, completely immobile. He looked like a tiny mummy. She placed a blanket over him to further protect him from the mild cold.

These morning walks were good for both of them. The fresh air helped her get ready for her workday at the inn, which would start with cooking and serving breakfast in less than an hour. Thomas seemed to enjoy the walks as well, cooing and gurgling to the rhythm of the wheels rolling on the road until it put him to sleep.

She usually walked to the church and back, which took about forty minutes. The road from the inn to the church was narrow and didn't have a sidewalk, but it was always quieter. She rarely continued farther east to the bustling activity surrounding the public beach, the boardwalk, the colorful villas, and the multiple boutiques that attracted tourists. Not in December, of course.

In December, all of Sainte-Luce-Sur-Mer was placid. But even in December, it was a small paradise to Melodie. All she needed was the Saint-Laurent, which she admired as the winter sun rose slowly, creating a pink and orange glow over the agitated waters. Even the church she saw in the distance, with its stone walls, sheet metal roof, and massive bell tower, wouldn't be nearly as majestic without the Saint-Laurent as its powerful backdrop.

She filled her lungs with cool sea air and thought of her tasks ahead. The one she dreaded the most was apologizing to Anais Bloom. She'd looked up her name in the computer, thinking her apology might not be as effective if she addressed the woman as Rich Uptight American Tourist. She didn't mind apologizing to people she cared about. She'd become quite an expert at it. But she wasn't looking forward to groveling in front of a stranger for the sake of business.

The stroller suddenly stopped and she walked right into the handlebar. "Damn shit, that hurt," she muttered as she brought a hand to her ribs. Thomas giggled and she took a peek at him under the blanket. "What's so funny? Are you laughing because your mama got hurt?" Thomas looked at her expectantly. She lowered her voice and bent closer. "Damn shit," she repeated. The boy laughed louder this time and she joined in. She'd found out a few days earlier that her favorite curse word made him laugh gleefully. She didn't know why, but she found it difficult not to abuse the power it had on him even though she knew it wasn't appropriate. "All right, little scoundrel, let's find out what's going on with your wheels."

She crouched and quickly found a small mass of salt stuck in one of the front wheels. They'd had a mix of snow and freezing rain during the night and the icy roads had been generously covered with salt. She checked the other wheels of the stroller for similar potential roadblocks when she heard a vehicle stop next to her. "Do you need help, Miss?"

"Certainly not from you," she answered without looking at the driver. She recognized Kevin's voice and was in no mood to talk to him. She got up and walked faster. The black pickup truck started again, only to park on the side of the road a few feet in front of her.

Every time she saw the forty-thousand-dollar truck, she was tempted to ask for child support, but she never did. She didn't want anything from Kevin. And she didn't want him to ask for anything in return.

She didn't regret having Thomas but she wasn't proud of the way she'd hooked up with her high-school sweetheart after ten years of exclusively dating women. They were sitting around a fire with friends one summer night and he'd put on the charm as he'd done periodically ever since she'd broken up with him after they'd graduated from high school. That night, she'd thought why not? She'd realized that perhaps she'd been fighting what was meant to be. She'd had her heart broken by a woman and she knew that couldn't happen with Kevin.

She'd become pregnant shortly after, which was not as shocking to her as it had been to Kevin since she forgot to take her contraceptive pill as much as she remembered. They'd moved in together during the pregnancy and a week after Thomas's birth, Kevin had left to work on a new construction site in Calgary. He was an ironworker and went where the job took him, often leaving for two or three months at a time. Melodie didn't mind that. She knew what she was getting into with Kevin. A few of her friends were married to ironworkers and it was simply a way of living, a comfortable way of living. Ironworkers worked hard but the pay was more than decent.

After two months of consistent weekly phone calls, a week went by without a call. She stopped by her in-laws' to check if they'd heard anything. She was worried. She found out he'd been back in town for five days, crashing in his parents' basement. He explained he wasn't ready to be a dad, and she'd given up the illusion that their little family might have been her destiny. Kevin never had the power to break her heart, perhaps, but he still succeeded in disappointing her. She felt like such an idiot every time she remembered it all, but all she had to do was look at Thomas to know that she'd been right. Her relationship with Kevin might have crashed and burned quickly, but it had left her with Thomas, and for that reason alone, she still believed it was meant to be.

Kevin got out of the truck with his broad shoulders, coy smile, messy beard and short dark hair. His bad boy good looks didn't have any effect on her anymore, but she had to admit she'd given her son good genes. "Come on, Mel, how long are you going to be mad at me?"

"As long as you remain the asshole you are," she replied, refusing to admit the rage she'd felt yesterday was already long gone to be replaced by mere annoyance. "You know, Kev, I never asked you for anything. No child support, no schedule to stick to. You're the one who begged for a weekend with Thomas."

"I know, and I really wanted to spend time with him, but something came up," he explained as he scratched the short beard on his neck.

She increased her speed so she could walk past him. "Not good enough. I had plans, you know. I had to cancel my night out because of you," she lied. "Do you think that's fair?"

"No," he continued as he walked by her side. "I know it wasn't fair, but I couldn't help it. I swear."

"Sure."

"Come on, Mel. I'm really sorry. Can you stop for a minute so I can see him?"

"No. And you have no right to ambush me on my morning walk. You know how important these walks are to me."

"Melodie, please."

She sighed, irritated, but stopped the stroller and Kevin crouched in front of it to see Thomas. "Are you sure he can breathe in that thing? He can't even move."

"He's fine, Kev. Would you rather see him freeze to death?"

"Hey little man," Kevin started. "I have an important secret for you." He got closer to Thomas and whispered, "Damn shit."

Thomas laughed, of course, and she had to bite her lip to keep from laughing too. She had to remain serious if she wanted to be credible when she chastised him.

"Stop! God, I should never have told you about that. What are we going to look like if those are his first words, huh?"

"Oh, don't be so dramatic. I'm sure he'll laugh at much more interesting things by the time he starts talking. He doesn't even know what we're saying," Kevin argued as he straightened up and faced her again.

"I guess you're probably right."

"What? What was that?" He grinned and pointed a finger to his right ear.

"You heard me, jackass," she replied as she swatted his hand. "Now let me finish my walk in peace. I have a big day ahead of me."

His smile vanished and he cleared his throat. "I'll let you go in a minute, but first there was something else I had to talk to you about. It's your dad."

"All right, what has he done now?"

Melodie resumed walking and Kevin followed. She was used to hearing about her alcoholic father's mishaps. She and her grandmother often had to help him out of sticky situations, and she'd grown to expect the worst.

"Apparently he hasn't worked in a while and he owes Aunt Judith two months' rent. She's about to throw him out. I convinced her to let me talk to you first."

She sighed and shook her head. Jerome Beaulieu had always managed to provide for her when she was growing up. He'd been a good father and she loved him dearly, but his alcoholism was now out of control. He worked small construction jobs, and he was known as a quick, talented, and meticulous worker. Unfortunately he was also known as the guy who didn't show up for work one or two days a week, and his unreliability always made him the first to be laid off toward the end of a project. "Well, thanks for letting me know. I'll talk to my grandmother about it, but please tell your aunt we'll call her. We'll pay what he owes her, of course."

"I figured as much. All right, then. Have a good day, Mel." He bent down toward Thomas before he added, "Bye bye, my little man. Damn shit." He ran away from her at the same time Thomas laughed.

"Yeah, you better run, Kevin Cloutier," she called through her own laughter. Better laugh than cry, she thought as she continued her walk toward the church, trying to clear her cluttered mind by focusing on the frantic waves the wind created on her beloved Saint-Laurent.

CHAPTER SIX

Ana had been sitting at a small wooden table for two since seven o'clock sharp. The innkeeper, who'd introduced herself as Yvonne, had given her a menu and had poured her a cup of coffee as soon as she'd sat down. She hadn't come back to take her order yet and it was seven fifteen. Ana didn't want to waste her day away sitting at this table. She'd planned to use weekends to explore Sainte-Luce-Sur-Mer, perhaps even Rimouski, but mostly to get acquainted with the Saint-Laurent River. She'd contemplated taking long walks on the beach and mentally reviewing the questions she wanted to ask during the meetings she'd scheduled for the coming week. She hoped these walks would allow her to meet other people she might interview for her research. None of that, of course, could happen while she was waiting to be served.

Fortunately the coffee was good. And she conceded that the dining room was charming. She didn't care for the wallpaper, covered in a pattern of dark and light roses, but she appreciated the effort to bring it to life by painting the ceiling in the same shade as the darker roses, a color she would call raspberry, which contrasted beautifully with the buttercream paint of the crown moulding. The area was open to the lobby, only partly separated from it by the bottom of the staircase. There were three other tables like the one she'd chosen, and two larger tables that could sit four people. She was alone this morning, but she figured other guests might come later. She wondered if anyone ever played the upright piano that sat against the wall of the staircase. It was a Baldwin piano and appeared to be at least a hundred years old. It made her itch to play for the first time in over a decade.

Ana brought her gaze back to the dog that had been sitting at the bottom of the stairs gawking at her. She called him over with a snap of her fingers, thinking she might as well pet him while she waited, but the dog didn't move. She guessed he was trained to never enter the dining room, which was a great idea, but she wished he'd also been trained to look elsewhere. His constant staring was disturbing. He was a beautiful dog, though. Probably a corgi, she thought, although she'd never seen one this color. His muzzle, neck, chest, and legs were white, but the rest of his body was a bluish grey with tan edges and small black spots. His eyes were bright blue, and they were still focused on her.

She averted her eyes from the furry stalker and turned back to her menu, as if she hadn't decided what she wanted yet. It was a simple piece of paper with three options printed in a common script font that could have been done on any home computer. Fortunately it was printed in both French and English. The choices were croissant served with homemade strawberry jam, Greek yogurt with granola and fruit, or eggs Benedict with sliced fried potatoes and fruit.

She heard the door of the lobby fly open even before she heard the damn bell and turned to see Melodie rush inside with the same baby Ana concluded was hers. Yvonne joined her and they exchanged a few words in French before Yvonne took the baby and Melodie walked past Ana with a polite smile before she disappeared behind the door Ana assumed led to the kitchen.

Yvonne put the sleeping baby in the bassinet and hurried to her table. "So what will you have this morning?"

"I'll try the eggs Benedict. And I'll have more coffee, please."

"Of course. And thank you for your patience."

"Sure," Ana replied curtly.

Yvonne went to the kitchen and came back with a fresh pot of coffee. She topped Ana's cup with the warm liquid, smiled, and went back to the kitchen. Ana wondered why Melodie wasn't helping and felt sympathy for Yvonne. She promised herself she'd leave her a generous tip despite the wait. A few minutes later the innkeeper came back with her plate. "Thank you," Ana said with a smile she hoped would erase her earlier impatience.

"My pleasure," she replied before she left again.

Ana took a bite of her eggs and hummed, pleasantly surprised. Eggs Benedict were her favorite breakfast meal, one she indulged in once a week. Unfortunately, she was often disappointed when she tried it in new places. The Hollandaise sauce was crucial to the success of the dish. If it was not made properly it could be bland and tasteless. Yvonne definitely knew how to make a tasteful Hollandaise sauce. There was a unique kick to it Ana enjoyed profusely until Melodie appeared.

"Sorry to bother you, Anais, but could I talk to you?"

"Sure, but call me Ana," she answered with hesitation. Melodie took the liberty to sit across from her at the table without asking or being invited, which made Ana raise her eyebrows in surprise. The woman really had some nerves.

"I wanted to apologize for my behavior yesterday. I'm afraid I didn't make a great first impression and I'm truly sorry about that."

She was going to tell her to forget about it, anything to get her away from her table so she could enjoy the rest of her breakfast in peace, but her cell phone rang, and of course Melodie answered it. She remained seated across from Ana as she engaged in an inflamed conversation over the phone. She recognized the words "no" and "Kevin" again. That Kevin sure seemed to know how to push Melodie's buttons, she mused before she realized she was listening to a private conversation that had nothing to do with her when all she wanted to do was to savor her eggs Benedict before they got cold. "Would you mind taking that somewhere else? I'm trying to eat," she snapped. Melodie rolled her eyes and huffed at her as if she were the rude one before she stood and returned to the kitchen.

Ana only had time to fork another bite before Yvonne approached her, "Would you mind if I sit with you for a minute?"

"No, not at all. Please do," Ana said sincerely, extending her free hand toward the unoccupied chair to emphasize her invitation. She'd always find time for a woman who could cook eggs Benedict this well.

"Did she at least have time to apologize before she took that phone call?"

"Kind of," Ana said after chewing and swallowing another bite. "I think we were interrupted before she had time to finish."

"Well, let me finish for her then. My granddaughter is a very impulsive young woman and you've probably guessed customer service isn't her strong suit. She's a hard worker though, and she has a good heart. Please don't let her behavior taint your opinion of us or this place."

"Don't worry, Yvonne. To be honest, I'd put up with a lot more of your granddaughter's lack of skills in customer service to eat more of your eggs Benedict."

Yvonne snorted a laugh at the compliment. "Oh dear, these are not mine. I can't cook. Never could. The menu was limited to the first two options before Melodie came on board. And she'd been making the homemade strawberry jam since she was twelve. It was my grandmother's recipe but my family's talent in a kitchen clearly skipped a generation. She's the chef in this family now. That said, I'm very happy she can make up for her rudeness with her cooking abilities."

Ana swallowed her bite with difficulty, as if admitting Melodie had redeeming qualities actually hurt. She considered her half-full plate for a few seconds but decided she didn't care who'd made this dish. It was simply too good not to finish it. "It certainly helps," she confirmed before she dug in with her fork.

"Great. I'll let you eat in peace then. I need to go get ready for my morning walk with Miller before he drills holes through you. Melodie will be here if you need anything else."

Ana narrowed her eyes in question and looked at the dog that was still staring at her, now with his tongue hanging out. "Is that Miller?"

"The one and only, yes. Sorry about the staring. I've never been able to break that strange habit out of him."

Yvonne stood and an idea popped into Ana's mind. An experienced business woman like Yvonne probably knew a lot of people, even some very influential people, Ana could interview for her research. "Would you mind some company?"

Yvonne turned and smiled. "You want to come for a walk with me and Miller?"

"Yes, I'd like to pick your brain about something I'm working on."

"Now you've piqued my curiosity. You're more than welcome to join us. Can we meet in the lobby in about fifteen minutes? I need to help Melodie clean up in the kitchen."

"I'll be there," Ana confirmed, looking forward to continuing her chat with the innkeeper. She decided Yvonne's career suited her perfectly. Her entire persona was welcoming and comforting. She guessed Melodie would inherit the inn someday, and she hoped for the sake of the family business that she would develop the same qualities. For now her talents in the kitchen far exceeded her hospitality.

After they finished the dishes in silence, Yvonne announced she was going for a walk with their guest and left the kitchen. Melodie knew she'd disappointed her again. She shouldn't have taken Kevin's call. She took a bottle of breast milk out of the fridge and placed it in a bowl of warm water. Thomas had never taken to her breast so this was the only way she could offer him the benefits of her milk. She hated the pump because it made her feel like a cow, but she wanted the best for her son.

She sighed with frustration thinking of Ana Bloom's smug expression when she dismissed her from her table. She shouldn't have taken the call, perhaps, but that arrogant bitch could have shown a little more understanding. She didn't have to act so superior, as if Melodie wasn't good enough to sit at her table. Did she think she was better than all of them because she wore a Ralph Lauren cashmere V-neck sweater over a perfectly pressed shirt at seven in the morning? She wondered if she'd wear the two-hundred-dollar sweater on her walk. Probably, since she'd judged it appropriate for breakfast at the White Sheep Inn. Melodie had no patience for rich judgmental jerks, and Ana Bloom definitely fit that category. She sprinkled a few drops of milk onto her wrist and, satisfied with its temperature, took the bottle to the lobby.

She stopped in her tracks when she reached the staircase, surprised to see Ana Bloom in the lobby, crouching down to pet Miller. She ignored her and went directly to the bassinet where Thomas was cooing patiently. "Are you hungry, beautiful boy?" she asked softly as she picked him up. She grabbed a burp cloth and a pillow she kept on a shelf under the reception desk and sat in the rocking armchair they left in the back corner of the lobby for this very purpose. She managed to get into a comfortable position, for she was used to juggling baby and feeding equipment. When Thomas took the bottle, she risked a look at the woman in the lobby.

She'd straightened from her crouching position and she was looking in their direction, smiling timidly at Thomas. "How old is he?"

"Six months," she answered shortly. Ana nodded. Melodie looked away before she could ask another question and tried to focus on Thomas. She didn't really want to start a conversation with her. She shook her head and took a deep breath, resigned. She had to try, didn't she? If only to make her grandmother proud. "His name is Thomas."

"He's really cute," Ana replied with a smile that communicated some warmth. Then again, babies had that effect on almost everyone.

"Thanks. I hear you're going on a walk with Miller and my grandmother?"

"I am, yes," Ana confirmed.

An awkward silence followed and Melodie wondered what was taking her grandmother so long. Miller's name inspired a thought and she decided to fill the uncomfortable silence with it. "She named him for Arthur Miller, you know, but we could pretend he was named after Henry Miller if you prefer."

Ana looked at her with puzzlement. "Why would I prefer that?"

"You know, Anais Nin and Henry Miller. The famous writers. There's a movie about them. No? Probably not your kind of literature, huh? A little too kinky?"

"I do understand the reference. I'm familiar with their writing, but I don't get it. I have nothing in common with Anais Nin, and as I've told you before, I prefer Ana."

"Never mind. It was just a thought," Melodie said with a sigh. Talking to her was like trying to have a conversation with a cloistered nun. "I'm surprised you know their writing, though. I wouldn't have pegged you as a fan."

"I didn't say I'm a fan. I simply said I know their work."

"Right. That makes more sense."

"Why is that?"

"Well, imagining you reading *Delta of Venus* would have been as shocking as that lock of hair standing straight up on your head right now. It would have been just as out of character."

Ana ran her hand through her hair but the said lock remained rebellious. That auburn mane was truly a wonder. So thick, wavy, and apparently untameable. Melodie figured it would fall to the woman's chin if it was straight and properly combed, but she enjoyed the way it stood out in every direction instead. "I've fought with my hair all my life," Ana explained with a bashful laugh. "I don't think I'll ever manage to conquer it."

"Don't you dare," Melodie protested.

"Excuse me?"

"Don't you dare try to change your hair. I like it that way. It's the only thing about you that's not so…" She let her voice trail off, realizing she was about to say too much. Again. Would she ever learn to think before she spoke?

"The only thing about me that's not so what?"

Of course she would push. She couldn't simply let it be, could she? "I don't know the best word for it. Rigid, maybe?"

Ana's features hardened and she swallowed. She zipped her North Face parka and declared in an incisive tone, "Well, on that beautiful compliment, I think I'll go wait for your grandmother outside. Enjoy the rest of your day, Melodie."

She opened her mouth to say something, to apologize at least, but the door closed behind Ana before she could think of something. She would never be able to make nice with such a frustrating woman, she concluded. Her grandmother would have to accept it.

As if on cue, Yvonne walked into the lobby wearing a warm jacket and holding Miller's leash. "She's not here yet? Good. I thought I'd kept her waiting."

"You have. She was here, but now she's waiting for you outside."

Yvonne squinted at her with admonishment. "What have you done now?"

"Nothing, I swear. I simply said I liked her hair." She knew her coy grin told another story and she expected to be scolded, but Yvonne simply shook her head as she clipped the leash to Miller's collar and joined their guest outside.

"I do like her hair, though," she said gently to Thomas, who kept sucking milk out of the bottle, blissfully unaware of his mother's latest faux pas.

CHAPTER SEVEN

As soon as they got to the beach and away from the road, Yvonne unclipped the leash and let Miller run free, throwing a blue rubber ball that he brought back as quickly as his overweight body allowed him. Ana smiled, amused by the dog's clumsy enthusiasm. The Saint-Laurent was as agitated as it had been at her arrival the day before, strong winds forcing the waves to break into foaming white crests. The sound of the wind and the waves was overwhelming, and she wondered how she would manage to have a conversation with Yvonne.

"So tell me, Ana, what it is you wanted to pick my brain about," Yvonne said loudly. She was obviously used to adjusting the volume of her voice around the fierce waters.

"Well," she said, matching Yvonne's volume, "I'm here to research the consequences of the storm surge of 2010, the measures that were taken to keep people from rebuilding close to the river and plans to help more people relocate in the future. I need to talk to as many people as I can to understand the situation. I was hoping you would give me an interview and perhaps you would know other people I should talk to."

"I see. That's certainly an issue that concerns all of us here. And you picked the right time, that's for sure. Everyone is worried about the high tides coming with the solstice next weekend and the complete absence of ice on the sea. We're all scared it will happen again."

"I'm afraid it will happen again, Yvonne. It's just a matter of time. Maybe not this year if the winds and the atmospheric pressure decide to cooperate, but it will definitely happen again. The most alarming part is that the next time it happens, it will probably be worse than it was in 2010. And the next time after that will be even worse." She noticed Yvonne slowed her pace and squeezed the blue ball in her hand. "I didn't mean to scare you. I'm sorry. I'm so passionate about this that I tend to alarm people. That's not my intention. I don't think alarming people is the best way to get them to act. Then again, it's hard to inform people about climate change and rising sea levels without alarming them."

"Oh no, don't worry," Yvonne reassured her. "I've heard all about the sea levels rising. What is it? Three millimeters a year?"

"At least, yes. But most scientists agree it will actually be much more than that if we don't stop using fossil fuels. Some say sea levels could be up to eight feet higher by 2100."

"Wow. Okay, I didn't know it could be that much, but I knew it was happening. I don't stop to think about it every day, but every time I do, I realize we have to do something about it. I even bought a piece of land on top of the hill over there," she said as she pointed south and away from the river. "You can't see it from here, but from there you do have a splendid view of the sea. My plan was to move the inn there. But it costs a lot of money to relocate a building like the White Sheep Inn, and although there are plans to help people relocate, we're not there yet. Besides, I worry about losing some of my customers. They come here for the sea, you know? Will admiring it from a distance be enough for them? I don't know."

"That's an understandable concern." Ana focused on Yvonne's hand as she was still holding the ball despite a frantic Miller running back and forth in front of her. She saw tremors in the older woman's hand, tremors that hadn't been there before. "Would you like me to throw the ball for you?"

"Would you, please?"

Yvonne handed the ball and Ana threw it as far as she could. Miller started running after it but stopped to sniff at the ground halfway to where the ball actually fell, used to his owner's throwing distance. He turned to them, puzzled, then turned around again and ran when he finally spotted the ball. Yvonne laughed. "I think he's in for a lot more exercise than he'd bargained for with you throwing it. If we did this every day, maybe he'd lose that extra weight the vet has been scolding me about for two years."

"I'd be happy to go on these walks with both of you while I'm here." Miller came back with the ball. He was panting, his tongue hanging. "But next time we'll bring water for him." She threw the ball again, but this time much closer to give him a break.

"That would be very nice of you, thank you. These damn tremors will only get worse with time," she said as she attempted to massage them away with her other hand. Ana didn't ask because she didn't want to intrude, but she didn't need to as Yvonne continued. "Parkinson's. That's why I started to train Melodie. I wanted to work with her as long as I could before the disease progresses too much. The inn will be hers when I can't do it anymore." She took a deep breath. Ana offered a timid smile. She didn't know what to say. "But enough about that. I'm still able to go out and enjoy walks for now. That's what matters, right?"

"Of course. And I'll throw the ball for Miller. We'll become great friends in the next few weeks, you'll see."

"I don't doubt it. And to answer your question, yes, I will give you an interview. We can do it during our walks. And I'll call people for you. I know a few people on the town council and if they can't help you, they'll know who can."

"Thank you so much, Yvonne."

"You're welcome. I'm glad you're interested in our community's fate. You're a scientist, I assume? Maybe you'll bring us solutions we haven't thought of yet."

"I'm an engineering geologist, yes, but I'm afraid you might not like my solution that much."

"Why?"

"Well, apart from stopping the use of fossil fuels as quickly as possible to limit damages, my solution is for governments, business owners, and citizens to get together and come up with a solid plan to relocate every home and every business farther from the river as soon as possible. The power of the oceans in general and of the Saint-Laurent River right here in Sainte-Luce-Sur-Mer is something we need to respect. The best thing for us to do is to get out of the way."

She closed her eyes and sighed deeply. "That's very sensible. It's not what many of us want to hear, so be prepared for some serious debates, but I for one agree with you. But do me a favor, will you?"

Ana turned to Yvonne, who looked at her with a mischievous grin. "Don't call the Saint-Laurent a river anymore. I know you don't have another word for *fleuve* in English, but river simply doesn't work. It doesn't do it justice," she explained as she stopped walking and turned toward the water to take a deep breath of wet, salty air. "Call it the sea. That's what we all call it here. *La mer.*"

"That I can do," Ana granted with a smile. She turned to the Saint-Laurent and nodded as the wind hit her face. Sea was a much better word for its magnitude.

CHAPTER EIGHT

Melodie and Thomas stayed in the only room located on the first floor of the inn. It was the largest of the guest rooms but it didn't have a view of the sea. It was right next to the kitchen and directly above the basement laundry room, so unpleasant ambient sounds were guaranteed. For these reasons, her grandmother had explained, they only let guests stay in that room when they didn't have any other vacancy and even then they warned them about the possible disturbance and offered it at a lower rate.

Melodie enjoyed her temporary living arrangements. Staying at the White Sheep Inn was strangely akin to coming back home. The only house she'd truly called home before was her grandparents' tiny saltbox house, which had been located less than a hundred feet west of the inn, right on the beach. She'd lived in several apartments in town with her parents, and then alone with her father, but the only place that had ever felt like a proper home was that blue house on the beach. Unfortunately it had been destroyed by the 2010 storm surge, and her grandparents had bought a duplex in the village. It had been a difficult transition, but at least they still had the inn.

She'd placed Thomas's crib next to her full-size bed and still had enough floor space to put down foam mat tiles for Thomas to play safely with his toys. She'd started with a four foot by four-foot area covered with checkered blue and green foam tiles, but now that Thomas was starting to crawl, she'd added a few more tiles. "Do you want the giraffe?" she asked him as she sat at one end of the cushy mat, wiggling the giraffe teether in her hand. That giraffe was his favorite thing in the world and she used it as bait to get him to move forward. So far he'd only managed to crawl backward, which was hilarious but sometimes frustrating for him. The time she spent on this foam mat playing with him was her favorite time of the day. He always made her laugh and impressed her almost on a daily basis with new skills. "Come on, baby, I know you want it."

She heard a knock on the door: two quick strikes, then a pause before one last, softer knock. "Come in, Mammie."

Yvonne entered and immediately picked up Thomas for a kiss. "Are you having fun playing with maman?" She kept making funny faces at him as she said to Melodie, "I set up the Tremblays in room three. They're staying for two nights so we'll have three breakfasts to serve tomorrow and the day after."

"Easy breezy."

"Speaking of breakfast, Ana really loved your eggs Benedict. You're really amazing in the kitchen. You'll earn us a new culinary reputation if you continue."

"Great. I'm glad I finally did something that woman likes."

Yvonne put Thomas back down on the mat and sat on the foot of the bed to watch them play. Melodie's heart sank. Not so long ago, her grandmother would have been happy to sit on the floor and play with them, but her body forced her to be more cautious now. "You should give her a chance, dear. She's very smart you know. And kind."

Melodie scoffed. "I don't doubt she's smart. Everything about her screams nerd. But kind, really? She seems so cold-hearted to me."

"You're wrong. While we were walking, she saw I was struggling with tremors in my hand and she offered to throw the ball for Miller."

"Oh Mammie, are you okay now?" Melodie asked as she automatically focused on her grandmother's right hand.

"Yes, don't worry. I took my medication and rested a little bit," Yvonne explained as she waved her hand dismissively. "You're missing the point."

"Well, youpidoo. She threw a ball. Give her the Nobel Peace Prize, why don't you?"

"You're not being fair, Melodie. She has a good heart. I'm old enough to sense these things. You should trust me. She's here to study ways to help people relocate away from the sea. You know, with the sea levels rising and all. She obviously cares about people."

"What? Are you kidding? She wants us to move away from the beach?" Melodie felt heat come up her body to the tips of her ears. The pressure and anger rose inside her much faster than any damn sea level could.

"Well, not only us, of course. She says the best thing we can do is get out of the way."

"That's ridiculous," she hissed. "We've always lived by the water. Who does that American bitch think she is, coming here to tell us we have to move away? She doesn't know this place. She doesn't know anything about us and she thinks she can impress us with her stupid relocation plans? Well, it's not going to happen. Mark my word. You can't let her put those ideas in your head, Mammie. Please tell me you won't," she argued, brandishing her index finger and the giraffe teether she was still holding at the same time.

"Calm down. She's not here to make us do anything. She's just here to study."

"That's how the stupidest plans and laws always begin. With damn studies."

"Shh, please let it go. Look!"

Melodie followed her grandmother's gaze to Thomas and Ana Bloom and her ridiculous ideas immediately left her mind.

Thomas was crawling toward her. He folded one leg on his side and pushed forward with his bare foot. Then he did the same with the other leg. "That's it, my love. You're doing it! Come and get the giraffe." Thomas kept crawling with the biggest smile on his face. He stopped short and reached as far as he could with his tiny arm. Melodie rewarded him by handing him the giraffe at last. She picked him up and held him tightly as he started chewing on the toy. "You did it, Thomas. Maman is so proud of you."

"Bravo, Thomas."

Melodie turned her attention back to her grandmother and saw tears of joy in the woman's eyes. She felt her own eyes well up with tears of pride. "I'm glad you were here for this big step."

"Me too," Yvonne replied as she squeezed the hand Melodie offered her. "Next he'll get on his hands and knees. That's when real trouble begins, you know."

"So I've heard," Melodie acknowledged as both women laughed together. She couldn't help but wonder how many big steps her grandmother would still be here to witness, and a different kind of tears soon mixed with her pride and laughter. Yvonne was the rock in their strange little family. She couldn't imagine not having her around. Thinking of her grandmother's strength brought to mind her father's weaknesses and she realized she hadn't shared the latest news yet. "Dad's been out of work for a while. He owes two months' rent. I told Kevin I would talk to you about it."

Yvonne sighed and dropped her shoulders, discouraged. "All right. Let me think about this for a day or two. I'll come up with something. If Kevin asks, just tell him we'll pay what he owes."

"Already done."

"Thank you. I think I'm going to head home if you don't mind."

"No, of course not. Go ahead. I'll take care of things here."

Yvonne bent down to kiss her cheek and Thomas's head before she left the room. She wanted to curse her father's lack of pride, but how could she when she was living in her grandmother's inn, no savings to her name? Savings she could have used to help out her father instead of passing on that responsibility to her grandmother. Yet again.

CHAPTER NINE

Ana came back to the inn around eight that night. She'd
gone to Rimouski to have dinner and had stopped by the church
for another walk by the sea—a solitary walk this time. It had not
been as beneficial as she'd hoped. In fact, the Saint-Laurent in
the dark was anything but comforting. The boisterous waves
became almost threatening when she couldn't see exactly where
they crashed or how far up the beach they crept. The beach was
covered with obstacles, and she'd stumbled upon several large
pieces of driftwood before she finally gave up. She would keep
enjoying the sea in the daylight, at least for now. She entered
the small hotel as quietly as she could and walked slowly toward
the staircase, not wanting to wake anyone. She'd noticed a new
car in the parking lot so she knew she wasn't the only guest
anymore.

"Could I talk to you for a minute?"

The question startled her and she gasped before she turned
around to see Melodie, sitting in the same rocking chair in the
back corner of the lobby where she'd seen her with Thomas
earlier. She was feeding him another bottle. "Oh hell, you

scared me half to death," she whispered so she wouldn't disturb the child.

"Sorry. There's no rocking chair in our room, so I always feed him here. Besides, I was hoping I'd see you come in." Melodie was not whispering but spoke softly.

"Do you stay here every night?" she asked as she approached Melodie and her son.

"Yes, this is our home. For now anyway."

"What about Yvonne and Miller?"

"My grandmother has her own place in the village."

"I see. Okay, well, I'm here. What did you want to talk to me about?"

"I'd like you to stop putting ideas in my grandmother's head about relocating away from the beach."

The volume of her voice had not increased and her tone was still soft and calm, yet she still managed to sound stern and antagonistic. Ana wondered how that was possible as she focused on not betraying her own defensive instincts when she replied. "Pardon me?"

"She told me about your conversation and your studies. I don't care what you're here to study, but don't go putting any ideas in her mind." This time she had not even looked at her. She'd kept a tender gaze on her son as she accused her of…of what exactly? Influencing an older woman?

"I'm not putting any ideas in your grandmother's mind, Melodie. She bought that land up the hill years ago, after all. I had nothing to do with that."

"What land?" Melodie jerked her head toward her and anger flashed through her narrowed blue eyes. They were even lighter than usual, like ice cubes in a glass of water.

"You didn't know about the land?" Ana was tempted to tell her all about Yvonne's plans to move the inn up the hill, but what would that achieve? She'd hurt her, but she'd betray Yvonne's trust in the same breath. And why was she tempted to hurt Melodie anyway? It wasn't worth it. "I think I'll let your grandmother tell you about it. But rest assured I have no evil plans to brainwash her in any way."

"Good," she said with a smile. "Because we're not going to run away from the sea. It's part of us. We're part of it. That's the way it's always been."

"Great. May I go to bed now?"

"Sure."

"Good night, Melodie."

"Good night, Anais." Ana cringed at the use of her first name but turned without saying a word. It was clear she insisted on calling her Anais to provoke her, but she wouldn't give Melodie the satisfaction to show it affected her. She'd almost made it to the staircase before Melodie spoke again. "This whole rising sea and climate change stuff, it's just a theory, after all, isn't it? Scientists don't even agree about it."

Ana closed her eyes and bit her lower lip as she shook her head. She sighed. No, she had not really said that, had she? As unnerving as she was, she seemed intelligent enough to know better. She couldn't really believe what she'd just said. *She's baiting you, Ana. Walk away. I can't.*

Instead, she rushed back to the rocking chair, and although she was still whispering, her tone and the rapid flow of her words betrayed her indignation. "You're right. Only ninety-seven percent of us scientists agree climate change is real, so I guess that's not enough." She watched Melodie feed Thomas with a satisfied smile, and she thought of the perfect argument. "Tell me something. If ninety-seven doctors out of a hundred told you formula was bad for your baby, would you keep feeding it to him? Would you think, oh well, the doctors don't all agree it's bad for him so it must not be that bad after all? What would you do, huh? Tell me."

Melodie took the empty bottle out of Thomas's mouth and stood, holding her son and looking at him lovingly. She walked by Ana and only then did she avert her eyes from her son to acknowledge her. She wiggled the bottle she was holding between her thumb and her index finger in front of her face. "For your information, this was breast milk. I don't feed my son formula." She then walked away and Ana watched until she disappeared in the dark hall. Ana promised herself she would never waste her time arguing with that woman again. It was too infuriating.

Melodie put Thomas in his crib and sat on the bed with a heavy sigh. "What's wrong with me?" she asked a sleeping Thomas. What was it about that woman that made her act this way? She'd never been one of those idiots who thought global warming and climate change were not really happening. She'd been environmentally conscious all of her life. She took pride in living in a community where each home had three garbage cans: one for trash, one for recycling, and one for composting. She always made sure everything they discarded went to the proper bin, driving her grandmother and her dad crazy at times. She used LED light bulbs, didn't drive her car unless she absolutely had to, and watched her usage of water and electricity as closely as possible. Yet she'd felt compelled to question the validity of Ana's studies. Why? Because she was threatening their way of living, that's why. She would do a lot for the sake of the environment, but she couldn't face the possibility that it might not be enough. That it might be too late. Ana had to be wrong about that.

She grabbed her tablet from the nightstand and opened the Internet. She typed in "solutions against rising sea levels" and started reading the results. She couldn't believe Ana was right about relocation being the best option, but she had to come up with better arguments than simply denying what she knew was really happening. She'd looked like an ignorant idiot, and that was not the impression she wanted to give Ana.

She also needed to find out about that land up the hill her grandmother had purchased. Why hadn't she heard about this before? More importantly, why was she learning of it from Ana Bloom?

CHAPTER TEN

Melodie walked into the lobby and tried to close the door behind her, but Kevin pushed it open with his hand and followed her inside. She took off her winter jacket and undressed Thomas. "Don't you dare wake him up. He always sleeps through breakfast and I want to keep it that way." She glanced at the dining room and saw that Ana was already seated at the same table she'd picked the day before, sipping on coffee. The Tremblays hadn't shown up yet, but it was barely past seven.

"Let me take him to my parents' this weekend and I won't wake him up."

He wouldn't let it go. He'd waited for her in the parking lot of the church and had followed her all the way back to the inn, badgering her about letting him take Thomas for the weekend. His brother and sisters were coming down from Montreal for a family gathering and he wanted to introduce them to Thomas. She clicked her tongue and sighed with resignation. "Fine. But you better not cancel on me this time."

"I won't. I promise," he replied with a cocky grin.

Yvonne met them in the lobby with a panicked expression on her face. "Where have you been?" she whispered. "I know you love these walks of yours but you can't be late every day. Breakfast starts at seven, not a quarter after."

"It's his fault. He keeps bothering me when all I want to do is walk in peace." She put Thomas in the bassinet while Yvonne turned her attention to Kevin.

"Good morning, Kevin. I trust you're doing well? And your parents?"

"We're all good, thanks Mrs. Beaulieu. And just so you know, I'm only bothering Melodie because she won't let me see my son."

"Is that so?" Yvonne said with a scowl toward Melodie.

"Oh shut up, Kev. I said you could have him this weekend, didn't I? Now let me through so I can get to the kitchen."

"Great, I'll call you at the end of the week."

"Sure, now get out of here." She pushed him out and closed the door behind him before she rushed to the kitchen, followed by her grandmother.

As soon as they were alone behind the closed kitchen door, Yvonne started nagging, following her around as she took out the ingredients she would need to make breakfast and lined them up on the counter top. "Why are you giving him such a hard time? Don't you want Thomas to know his father?"

"Of course I want him to know his father. But I also wanted to make sure he doesn't cancel on me again. He has to take this seriously."

"As seriously as you take our guests? Ana has been waiting for fifteen minutes."

Melodie took a deep breath and turned to her grandmother. She placed her hands on the shorter woman's shoulders and looked her in the eye when she said in a firm but reassuring tone, "Mammie, I'm here now. Everything will be okay. Do you know what she wants yet?"

"No, but I'll go find out."

"Perfect."

She took out her favorite pan and she was ready to go when Yvonne came back. "She wants the yogurt today. The Tremblays just came down so I'll come back with their order in a minute." Yvonne went back to the dining room and Melodie grabbed a tulip shaped glass dish in which she put Greek yogurt and a generous layer of fresh berries before she sprinkled her homemade granola mix on top. She handed the dish to her grandmother when she came back, asking for eggs Benedict and a croissant with homemade jams for the Tremblays.

She prepared their orders and followed Yvonne through the kitchen door when she took the plates full of food to their table. Satisfied to see that Ana was still seated and slowly eating her breakfast, she hurried to her room to get the article she'd printed the night before. She stopped at Ana's table on her way back to the kitchen. "No eggs Benedict today?" she asked politely.

"No. They're delicious, but their richness is something I indulge in only once a week."

"Wow, it must be exhausting to be in control like that all the time." She closed her eyes. Why did she have to say that? Why was it that everything this woman did got on her nerves? Why should she care if she ate yogurt every morning for the rest of her life?

"Not really. It merely takes discipline."

"Discipline, right." She successfully swallowed every snippy remark she was dying to let out in that moment and focused on the reason why she'd stopped at her table in the first place. "Anyway, I wanted to give you this article I found last night. I'd like to know what you think about it." She put the article she'd printed on both sides of two pieces of letter-size paper on the table.

"Okay. I'll take a look after breakfast."

"Great, thanks." She managed to smile at Ana before she went to clean up the kitchen. When their guests were done with their plates, Yvonne joined her. They got into their routine without talking. Yvonne did dishes and Melodie prepped food for the following morning. "Are you going for a walk with her today?"

"Yes."

"You can go and get ready if you want. I can finish on my own."

"Are you sure?"

"Of course. Sorry I was late. It won't happen again."

"Don't make promises you can't keep," Yvonne said with a wink as she removed her apron and hung it on a wooden hook on the wall. Melodie was relieved to see she'd calmed down and her sense of humor was back.

Yvonne was about to open the kitchen door when Melodie dared asking the question that had been burning her tongue all morning, "Is it true you bought a piece of land up the hill?"

"Yes," her grandmother answered tentatively without turning around.

"Why? Did you want to move the inn up there?"

Yvonne sighed and finally turned to her. "Yes. I bought it after our house was ruined. I thought the government would help us relocate. I wanted to save the history in this place, Melodie. Our family history. This inn means more to me than the land it's on. You understand?"

Melodie nodded. She did understand, but she couldn't imagine the White Sheep Inn anywhere else. "But what is this place without the sea, Mammie? People don't come here for squeaky beds, you know."

It was her grandmother's turn to nod. "You might be right. It's too late for me to make this happen anyway. The land up the hill will eventually be yours too, though. So it will be up to you to decide. Maybe we could go see it together and I can explain what I had in mind?"

"I guess that wouldn't hurt," she agreed with a smile. Yvonne squeezed her hand and left the kitchen. She owed it to her to at least listen to what she'd envisioned for the future of the White Sheep Inn, especially now that she was reassured she'd made those plans long before Ana Bloom came into their lives.

Ana took the article to her room and read all of it as she lay in bed. She had time before she had to meet Yvonne for their walk with Miller and the article wasn't long. It discussed several scientists' ideas to protect the community against storm surges. It talked about building a protective wall in a mix of steel, stone, and concrete. The material would be strong enough to resist storm surges, yet flexible enough to allow more creative shapes that could be inspired by nature. An engineer even mentioned the possibility of adding turbines to the structures, giving them another purpose by producing green energy. These were not bad ideas, but they were not new to Ana. They wouldn't change her mind and her preference for the retreat strategy.

The reason why she'd read the entire article was not for its informative nature, but because Melodie had given it to her. She didn't go as far as taking it as a peace offering. On the contrary, Melodie was clearly trying to convince her that there were better solutions than to move away from the beach. The gesture was argumentative, but it gave her hope, nonetheless. It was a way to open an intelligent dialogue. And more importantly, it proved that Melodie had an environmental conscience and knew climate change was real. She'd gone through the trouble of doing her own research and coming up with valid arguments, which earned her Ana's respect. "So there's a brain behind those piercing blue eyes after all," she concluded as she rolled the article in her hands and an unexpected warm current traveled through her veins.

CHAPTER ELEVEN

"What kind of dog is he? His markings are very unique," Ana asked as she threw the ball for Miller again. She propelled it farther than Yvonne did, but not quite as far as she could. The dog was getting used to her distance and found the ball easily.

"He's a Cardigan Welsh Corgi. And that coloring is called blue merle. I fell in love with him the minute I saw him."

"Have you always had a dog?" Ana remembered wanting a dog as a child, but her mother travelled too much to be bothered with an animal. A dog would force them to stay put, she'd always tell young Ana. Perhaps that was the real reason she wanted one so badly. Staying put was her childhood dream, but her mother's career as a struggling theatre actress didn't allow it.

"No, Miller is my first pet. I never thought I'd want a dog, but Melodie showed me a picture of these puppies a friend of hers had. She knew I needed company after my Raymond died, and falling in love with another man was out of the question. I couldn't see myself sharing my life with another human being.

Training Miller was much easier." Yvonne laughed and she joined, enjoying her light humor.

After Miller brought the ball back a few times he panted and Ana took a bottle of water out of her backpack. It was a special kind of bottle she'd purchased at a pet shop in Rimouksi the day before. It had a foldable dispenser the clerk had promised would make it easy for a dog to drink. She bent down and Miller lapped water out of the dispenser, proving the clerk had been right. Yvonne laughed again. "Oh wow, isn't that convenient? Where did you get that? Do you have a dog at home?"

"No, I got it for Miller. If we're going to help him lose that extra weight we need to keep him hydrated, don't we? You can have it when I leave."

Ana straightened up and Yvonne squeezed her arm. "That's so thoughtful of you. Thank you." Her eyes were the same color as Melodie's, but there was so much more warmth in her gaze. She seemed genuinely grateful, and Ana felt warmth in her cheeks despite the cold sea air.

"It's nothing, really." She wasn't used to gratitude. She'd taken care of her mother in one way or another for as long as she could remember, but Constance had never shown the same appreciation Yvonne so easily communicated through her words, her eyes, and her smile. She shook her head. She'd barely thought about her mother since the funeral, yet this short walk with Yvonne had surfaced memories of her twice already. What was that about? She didn't want to think about Constance. She focused on the sea, which was slightly calmer today. The frigid wet air hit her face, and she heard the sound of her boots on the thin layer of snow that had fallen overnight.

"This is it," Yvonne declared. "This is where our little house used to stand." She stood in one spot of the beach, opened her arms and slowly pivoted. Ana looked carefully, but there was nothing left of the house Yvonne had described before she decided to show her its site. Ana didn't know why she'd imagined there would be some sign the small blue home had once been here, but it had completely vanished. She looked at the older woman and smiled with compassion. She smiled back, but the warmth in her eyes had been replaced with sadness. "I don't want this to happen to the inn. But it will, won't it? If we don't move it?"

Ana nodded. She didn't want to confirm Yvonne's fears with words, but she couldn't lie to her. "Yes, eventually," she said at last. Yvonne sighed and stood in silence, looking at the empty space around her. Ana understood she was recreating her home in her mind. She could still see it. Miller sat patiently as Ana waited, holding the ball in her hand. When Yvonne finally resumed walking, she threw the ball and the dog ran to fetch it. They took several steps before Ana dared speaking again. "Did the inn sustain any damages in that storm?"

"Nothing serious, thank god. It's farther up the beach as you know. Smaller homes that were closer to the water like our house took the biggest hit. The inn got a bit of water in the basement but that's all. But I'm not stupid. I know the next storm won't need to be much worse for..." She didn't finish her thought. They both knew what could happen in the next storm. "Melodie said she'd come to see the land I bought. Maybe I can convince her to do what I'd planned to do."

"Maybe."

Ana doubted there was any possibility Melodie would ever consider moving the inn away from the beach, but her grandmother knew her better. She hoped she was right.

"There's still time, right? She'll understand it's the best thing to do sooner or later."

"There's still time, yes. Although it's hard to estimate how much."

"You should talk to her."

Ana scoffed. "I think your chances are much better than mine. I have a feeling your granddaughter doesn't care much for me or for my beliefs."

Yvonne slid her arm under hers and insisted, "She's stubborn and she says whatever goes through her mind, but she's smart. She'll understand if you explain it to her. Will you please at least try?"

Ana glanced at the woman with whom she was now walking arm in arm, and she couldn't bring herself to say no. "Okay. I'll try."

When they got back to the hotel, Melodie was behind the reception desk holding Thomas and going through a pile of papers that looked like bills. The boy sat in her lap, chewing on a toy giraffe and drooling all over his mother's hand. "Mrs. Vezina called. She won't be able to babysit while we go to your doctor appointment tomorrow afternoon, so I guess we'll have to take him with us." Melodie spoke to Yvonne as if Ana wasn't in the room, but she spoke English, so she obviously was aware of her presence. Ana started toward the stairs, but for some reason she wanted to hear the rest of this conversation. Maybe she could help. She crouched down to offer Miller the water that was left in her special bottle and she listened quietly.

"Don't be silly. With the waiting time it could take a couple of hours. That's too much time for a baby to sit in a doctor's office, even one as good as our Thomas," Yvonne replied as she hurried to take her jacket off so she could take Thomas in her arms. Melodie grabbed a washcloth from the desk and wiped the boy's mouth before she dried her own hand. "I can go to my appointment alone. You stay here with him."

"No, I've already told you I want to be there. I have questions for your doctor and I think it's important we both hear what she has to say."

"How are you going to be able to focus if you have Thomas with you? No, I'll go alone. It's better this way."

Ana was tempted to suggest she could take Yvonne to her appointment, but finding herself in another doctor's office to hear about another illness was not something she felt strong enough to do. She didn't want to be reminded of Constance and it had happened too often already in Yvonne's presence. Besides, it was Melodie's place, not hers. "I could stay with Thomas," she proposed instead, surprising herself as much as the other two women.

"Oh Ana, it's nice of you to offer, but we can't impose. Don't you have people to see for your research?" Yvonne protested.

"My first appointment is on Tuesday. I'm free tomorrow."

"But do you know anything about babies?" Melodie asked bluntly.

Although Ana usually found her directness somewhat abrasive, she smiled. She couldn't blame her for asking. After all, how could Melodie know she'd spent her teenage years taking care of younger kids travelling with Constance's theatre company? It was true she hadn't held a baby in almost fifteen years, but she figured she'd remember what to do. "I think I can manage for a few hours."

"I don't doubt you can," Yvonne replied, apparently embarrassed by her granddaughter's reaction, "but are you sure you want to?"

"Absolutely. Thomas and I will have a great time."

"Great, that solves the problem then, right?" Yvonne turned to Melodie, whose furrowed brow still showed scepticism. "We could stop by that place I wanted to show you after the appointment."

Melodie finally sighed in resignation. "All right then, but I'll give you my cell phone number. I want you to promise you'll use it if you have any question at all."

"I promise."

"Thank you," she said in a whisper. It seemed it almost hurt her to show gratitude, but when she smiled, Ana was struck by the beauty of her features. It was the first genuine smile she'd seen on her face and it moved her more deeply than a smile should.

She didn't know if it was because she appreciated Yvonne so much and couldn't help but hope their resemblance was more than physical, but it was as if she could suddenly see past Melodie's bad attitude and frequent rudeness. She realized she was a great mother and a caring granddaughter, and she thought perhaps trying to talk to her about her study and the retreat strategy was not a complete waste of time after all. Besides, she'd promised Yvonne she'd try. So instead of excusing herself and going to her room, she did exactly that. Try. "I read that article you gave me. It was very interesting. You said you wanted to know what I thought about it so would you like to talk now?"

"I'd love to, but I can't now. I have to get all this paperwork in order before the accountant comes in the morning. What about tomorrow when we get back?"

Ana took a look at the pile of papers on the desk and understood that Melodie truly had a lot of work on her plate and was not simply feeding her an excuse to brush her off. She would not have imagined she was responsible for the inn's paperwork, but she was pleasantly surprised. She was also relieved this laborious task didn't fall on Yvonne's shoulders. "Tomorrow will be fine. Good luck with all of this," she said as she pointed a finger to the desktop.

Melodie nodded and smiled again before she turned back to the papers in front of her. "I'll take Thomas so you can focus on what you're doing," Yvonne said before she followed Ana to the stairs. "Same time tomorrow morning?"

"Yes, of course," Ana replied.

"Thank you for trying," she whispered so Melodie couldn't hear. "I'm sure she'll listen to you."

"We'll find out," Ana answered in a low voice. "She seems to learn quickly. She's already doing the paperwork for the inn, I see."

"Oh god, she's been doing that for years. Ever since she got her degree in administration. I was so happy when she offered to take that task off my hands. I hate desk duties." She mimicked an exaggerated shudder to express her disgust and Ana chuckled. "Well, I'll see you tomorrow then."

"Right. See you tomorrow." Yvonne disappeared down the hall with Thomas in her arms and Miller at her heels. Ana remained alone at the bottom of the stairs, observing a focused Melodie at work. A caring granddaughter indeed, she mused before she finally turned and climbed the stairs.

CHAPTER TWELVE

"Take a look at that view," Yvonne said with enthusiasm, her arms open toward the breathtaking panorama. They were standing on top of the hill and watched as the Saint-Laurent ran furiously at their feet. Their unobstructed view allowed them to see the church and colorful villas in the foreground, the beach, the sea, and the North Coast on the other side, so far away that it could be mistaken for a darker shade of blue sky on the horizon. She couldn't deny it was a beautiful site. "And the land is big enough to build a large gazebo in the back where people could enjoy the view. We could have flower gardens with stone paths leading to strategically placed benches or picnic tables where guests could watch the sun set. We could even perform weddings. Can you imagine?"

Melodie tried to picture her grandmother's plans as her hair hit her face, violently blown by the wind. She used her hands to hold her curls back so she could better admire the imaginary scene Yvonne painted. "It would be amazing, you're right. But I'm not convinced it would be better than what we have now. A gazebo is wonderful, but does it beat being able to come out of your hotel and finding yourself right on the beach?"

Yvonne held her arm as they both faced the Saint-Laurent. "It's not a matter of finding a better place, dear. You and I both know we already have the ideal spot for a hotel. It's a matter of moving to a different spot before the sea takes it all away."

"But we won't let that happen, Mammie. I've read about it and there are dozens of ideas to help protect us from the sea. Running away is not the only option we have. If I thought it was, I would agree with you, but there are scientists coming up with other solutions all the time. Why not have faith in them?"

"Because all of those ideas are costly and governments haven't even allocated money and resources to make them happen yet. Meanwhile we don't know how much time we have before a bigger storm hits us and washes out the inn like the last one washed out our home. Do you really want to take that risk? Do you really want to put our fate in other people's hands?"

She watched her grandmother walk away before she could answer, massaging her right hand. The doctor had told them it was likely the medication would no longer suffice to manage the tremors. She'd suggested surgery, which Yvonne had promised to consider. It wasn't surprising she didn't want to depend on other people for the future of her inn. She was already losing control over her own body. Melodie turned to the sea one last time to take in the view before she followed her grandmother to the car she'd parked on the side of the road.

"I think I'll ask your dad to move into the duplex with me," Yvonne declared as they climbed into the small Honda Civic.

"What? Don't do that. He'll drive you crazy."

"I'll do my best to drive him crazy first so he gets a job and gets his own apartment again." Yvonne chuckled but her eyes showed nothing but concern. "I can't afford to keep paying for his apartment, dear. And if—no, when—something happens to me, I don't want you to inherit that responsibility. So I'll try again."

"Try what, Mammie?"

"To make a man out of my son."

"He's already a grown man, though. He's an irresponsible man, maybe, but he's an adult and it's too late to change him. You'll make yourself sicker trying."

"We'll see."

Melodie started the car and drove away. There was no point arguing when her grandmother had made up her mind. She could only hope her father wouldn't kill her before her time.

Ana paced nervously in the lobby as she held a crying Thomas in her arms. She'd tried bouncing up and down, rocking back and forth. Nothing worked. They'd had a good time until about ten minutes ago. They'd played on the foam mat Melodie had placed in her room, exploring each toy thoroughly. There were so many new kinds of toys Ana had never seen before. "Please laugh again, baby. You're so much cuter when you laugh." The first time she'd made him laugh, she'd felt her heart swell with pride. She'd simply crossed her eyes and stuck out her tongue and he'd exploded in laughter. She'd repeated the grimace so many times her eyeballs hurt, but she'd do it again if it could keep Thomas from crying. She'd changed his diaper, but that didn't help. He was hungry.

Melodie said they wouldn't be gone long enough for Ana to feed him so she'd left no instructions about meals. She stared at her cell phone on the desk, wondering if she should call her, but she didn't want to disturb them if they were still in the doctor's office. Then she remembered the bottle Melodie had arrogantly held in her face as she'd announced it contained breast milk. She almost ran to the kitchen, still holding Thomas tightly. Surely there would be another bottle in the fridge. She only needed one. She opened the door and sighed with relief. "Bingo!"

She went through the cupboard until she found a large bowl and let water run until it was warm enough to fill the bowl. She put the cold bottle of milk in the warm water and brought her attention back to Thomas, who'd stopped crying. He looked at her with anticipation, making a suction movement with his little heart-shaped mouth. She sprinkled milk on her forearm. Still too cold. "Hang in there, baby. There's a bit of a line at the door but I've heard the food is worth the wait."

Thomas looked at her with big, round blue eyes. His dark hair was almost as messy as hers, sticking out in every direction. She smiled at him and he smiled back. He was truly adorable when he wasn't crying. She dared a grimace again. She thought it was working when he giggled for a few seconds before he screwed his face into a grimace of his own and started crying again. "All right. I know, I know. It's time for food, not for funny faces." She tested the milk again and decided it was warm enough. She offered it to Thomas who sucked on it with gusto as she walked back to the lobby and sat in the rocking chair.

She wished she had the pillow she'd seen Melodie use before, but she'd have to manage without it. Her hands were full, and she couldn't move. How did Melodie do it? She found a semi-comfortable position and stared at him as he drank from the bottle. He placed his small hand over hers and her throat tightened. As a teenager, taking care of younger kids had been nothing but a burden. Playing with Thomas and feeding him today was a completely different experience. It was as close as she'd ever come to understanding maternal instincts. This little boy tugged at her heart, at her deepest emotions.

"Oh thank god you found a bottle." Ana jumped, startled by Melodie's voice. She was so focused on Thomas she hadn't heard the women come in. Not even the doorbell. She looked up at Melodie and then saw Yvonne smiling at her with tenderness. "I'm so sorry. I was sure we'd be back before feeding time. I can take over from here."

"No, I'd like to finish if you don't mind, but I'd like that pillow you usually have though."

Melodie grabbed the pillow from under the desk and installed it under Ana's arm. "Here you go," she whispered.

"Thank you," Ana mouthed.

She took a step back and watched quietly as the scientist fed her son and they stared at each other. She saw Thomas's little hand on top of Ana's pale skin, saw her slender fingers around the bottle. The scene moved her. She smiled and swallowed. No, it troubled her. It forced her to see Ana as more than a threatening scientist. It made her see the woman. It gave her a glimpse of the kind heart her grandmother had mentioned. Admitting there was another side to Ana was annoying enough, but what really perturbed her was that she felt a visceral pull to that new side of her. She took a deep breath and squared her shoulders. She couldn't be attracted to any part of Ana Bloom. "If you're okay with it, I'll go change."

"No problem. We're good here." Ana turned from Thomas long enough to smile at her and there was so much warmth in that smile that she felt her face heat up. And since when did she have such deep green eyes? She'd never even noticed the color of her eyes before. She had to get away.

"Go ahead, dear. I'll stay with Ana."

"Thanks," Melodie managed to say before she rushed to her room. She hurried to take off her winter jacket as unbearable heat washed over her. What was happening to her?

"You're a natural. Have you ever thought about having children of your own?" Yvonne asked as she took Thomas. She wasn't entirely sure what to do after he finished his bottle, so she watched as Yvonne placed a burp cloth on her shoulder and held him upright against her chest, gently patting his back.

"I did at one time, but then my career took over."

"I see. It's not too late, though. Do you have a husband or a boyfriend waiting for you back home?"

Danielle immediately popped into Ana's mind, as she did every time she was asked questions about her love life. Those four years with Danielle had been her only experience with love. "No, I don't have anyone. I had a partner once. A woman. But that was a long time ago. My career really does keep me busy." She watched for Yvonne's reaction, hoping she wouldn't be offended by her declaration, but refusing to let her continue to believe anything other than the truth.

She didn't really peg the older woman as homophobic, but she wasn't expecting the wide smile she offered either. "Well, I'm sure you'll meet the woman for you sooner than later. You have too much to offer to remain single."

"That's kind of you, thank you," she replied. The truth was that love had been erased from her list of priorities the day Danielle had left her. Actually, if you asked Danielle, she'd probably say love had never been among her priorities at all. They spent the last several months of their relationship arguing about one thing and one thing only: Ana spent too much time at work and not enough time with her. Their romance had gone smoothly at first but once Ana had plunged into research on climate change, she'd become obsessed. In the end Danielle concluded she wasn't strong enough to compete with the planet. Ana had realized she'd been right, of course, but it was too late.

"Did you know Melodie is like you?" Yvonne asked, suddenly interrupting Ana's thoughts.

"What do you mean?"

Thomas was now asleep, his head heavy on Yvonne's shoulder, and she put him in the bassinet before she answered. "She's a lesbian."

Ana was shocked at the revelation, but even more at the fluttering it caused in her stomach. "Really? But what about Kevin?"

"Oh, don't get me started on that. I would say it was a big mistake, but it gave us our little Thomas so I guess the best I can say is that it was a good mistake."

"But then how can you be so sure she's a lesbian? I'd say she's at least bisexual, because a mistake like Kevin would never even be a possibility for me."

"Fine, call it what you want. All I know is that the only time I've seen my granddaughter truly in love was with a woman."

"Oh," was all Ana could answer. She didn't know how to react to that piece of information. She didn't like that it affected her at all, and she didn't understand why it did. Yvonne massaged her hand and it gave her the perfect excuse to change the subject. "How did it go at the doctor's?"

"I'll probably need surgery. The meds can't completely control my tremors anymore. That said, the surgery is not guaranteed to succeed either." She pinched her lips together and closed her eyes. Ana had never seen her so disheartened.

"But it might help, right?"

"Yes, it might."

"Hope is always good," she said as she offered a compassionate smile. Yvonne returned her smile and squeezed her hand.

"Yes, always. And speaking of hope, I think Melodie liked the land up the hill." She winked and Ana chuckled. At least she remained hopeful about something.

Melodie came back to the lobby wearing jeans and a relaxed floral-print, shirred blouse that seemed too light for the season and definitely showed too much cleavage. Ana actively avoided staring at the smooth uncovered flesh, a task that required focus and dedication. "Oh, he's sleeping," she noted as she glanced at the bassinet. "Would you mind covering the reception desk while I go get a load of laundry started?" she asked Yvonne.

"I don't mind but I can take care of the laundry, dear. I thought you and Ana had something to talk about."

Ana took the hint and continued, "That's right. We were going to discuss that article you gave me."

"Oh, right. Could we postpone that? I have a bit of a headache right now."

"Sure, no problem."

"Thank you. And thank you for taking care of Thomas today."

"It truly was my pleasure." Ana barely had time to finish her sentence before Melodie disappeared, as if she couldn't get away from her fast enough.

CHAPTER THIRTEEN

Melodie was grateful the Tremblays had left the day before, and Ana only wanted the Greek yogurt with fruit and granola again. A reasonable breakfast for a reasonable woman. She carefully shook her head. Yesterday she would have described Ana as a control freak. Now she was reasonable. She was glad for the simple breakfast request because she'd barely slept, and her morning walk had failed to energize her the way she'd hoped. The headache she'd faked to avoid her talk with Ana had become reality. Karma, she figured. She popped two Tylenols and massaged her forehead, starting with the space between her eyebrows and slowly going up to her hairline. Her grandmother joined her in the kitchen after serving their only guest. "What's wrong? Did Thomas keep you awake?"

"Yeah, kind of." She didn't want to admit what had really kept her awake were thoughts of Ana mixed with memories of Aurelie. She hadn't thought of Aurelie in months, and she didn't understand why she was coming back to haunt her nights now. She'd lost enough because of that woman already. She'd lost a good job as office manager for an established local manufacturer of kitchen cabinets, but that wasn't even the worst of it. She'd also lost her mind, her dignity, and her heart. She certainly didn't need to lose more sleep over her. Why did her brain get Ana and Aurelie mixed together? Was it some kind of warning?

"Are you going to have that talk with Ana today? It should be pretty quiet around here."

"If I feel better, yes."

Yvonne made a fresh pot of coffee and the noise of the coffee grinder soon became unbearable. Melodie thought she was going to vomit. "You know that gaydar thing you've told me about before?"

Melodie opened her eyes to see her grandmother's mischievous grin. She vaguely remembered explaining the expression years go. "Mhm," she simply offered, grateful the coffee grinder had finally stopped its din.

"Well has your gaydar been detecting anything for the past few days?"

"Mammie, I might have fun playing your game if my head wasn't about to explode, but since I'm totally miserable, could you please tell me what you're trying to say?" The sudden pounding in her chest told her she already knew, but she needed her grandmother to confirm it at once.

"Ana is a lesbian," she whispered with exaggerated articulation.

It made complete sense, and in other circumstances she might have been happy to hear the news, but all she could think of now was that it made Ana even more dangerous. It explained her reaction to seeing her with Thomas yesterday. It even justified it, perhaps, but it made the warmth that had travelled through her body even more threatening. Because having an affair with the enigmatic scientist was now within the realm of possibilities, and she had to remain strong to keep it from happening. They were two diametrical opposites. It would never work. More importantly, Ana was not in Sainte-Luce-Sur-Mer to stay. She'd be gone as soon as her damn research was done. She'd tasted temporary with Aurelie. She didn't want a second bite. Her brain was definitely trying to warn her, and she would listen for once.

"Well, what is it? Did you know or were you as clueless as I was?"

"Clueless," she answered, although it was not entirely true. Her body had figured it out the day before.

"I knew it. So are you going to be nicer to her now?"

"Why? I should be nice to her because she's gay? That doesn't change the fact that she's here to cause trouble, Mammie."

"She's not here to cause any kind of trouble," Yvonne retorted before she sighed with frustration. "You can be so stubborn sometimes." She grabbed the pot of coffee and left the kitchen. Melodie resumed massaging her forehead, repeating to herself that Ana was indeed nothing but trouble.

* * *

Ana picked up the ball Miller had brought back and threw it again. Although it had only been a few days, it felt like they'd walked together for years. They were used to each other's rhythm and their game of fetch had become a well choreographed, pleasant activity. Ana had also become astute to Yvonne's subtle changes of pace and easily adapted to them. These morning walks were quickly becoming her favorite part of the day, although she also wished she could spend time with Thomas again after their afternoon of bonding. And she had to admit being in the same room with Melodie was getting more tolerable. She still feared she could lash out for no apparent reason, but she'd become more than a ticking bomb.

Behind her attitude hid a woman Ana was surprised to realize she wanted to know better. The woman who'd generously helped her grandmother manage the inn for years and who was such an attentive mother to Thomas. The woman whose rare, genuine smiles induced inexplicable physical reactions in her. The woman whose beauty was more difficult to ignore.

"So you have your first interview today?"

"Yes, this afternoon. Professor Hubert from the university. He specializes in geomorphology and he was my first contact here actually. I saw him speak at a conference in New York and that's how I first heard of this place. We've exchanged emails since then, but I can't wait to have a more in-depth conversation with him."

"Why here? There are so many places, much larger and better known cities in your own country that face similar challenges."

"That's a question I've had to answer many times already," she said with a chuckle.

"Oh, I'm sorry. You don't have to answer..."

"Oh no, don't worry," Ana quickly interrupted to reassure Yvonne. "I get asked often because it's a good question. My official answer is that there are plenty of people working on those big American cities already. The retreat strategy I favor is not something they want to hear. Millions of people live by the ocean and are at risk, not to mention businesses and the entire stock market in Manhattan. Leaving is a daunting option. I understand that. But when I heard Professor Hubert say that it was a strategy that was seriously discussed here, I immediately wanted to be part of these discussions. I'm convinced everyone needs to move away from the rising seas, and I want to work with people who have the same beliefs. So there. That's the long, official answer."

"It's a good one. But I'm curious about the unofficial answer now?" Yvonne glanced at her and offered one of the mischievous grins she was quickly growing fond of.

"I've never told anyone about the unofficial answer." She hesitated, but realized Yvonne was the perfect person to confide in. "Professor Hubert included videos and pictures of Sainte-Luce-Sur-Mer in his presentation, and something happened in me. It was like a deep attraction I couldn't ignore. I had to come here. I can't explain it with scientific facts or logical reasoning. I just had to come."

"That's the best reason to do anything, if you ask me. Your guts know more than your brain. I know that's hard to believe for a scientist like you, but try to remember that."

Ana nodded and Yvonne took her arm. They walked in silence for a few minutes. Ana broke their contact to give Miller some water and throw the ball again. She'd been dying to ask Yvonne about the woman Melodie had been in love with, but she didn't know how to bring it up. It was personal, and it wasn't her business, yet she was curious. Yvonne would tell her to take the plunge, wouldn't she? "How did you react when you found out Melodie was in love with a woman?"

If Yvonne was surprised by the question she didn't let it show. "I'd never seen her so happy, so I could only be happy for her in return."

"That's great. I'm sure she appreciated your support."

"Don't get me wrong. I wasn't always so enthusiastic about Melodie's preference for girls. When she started dating girls after high school, I thought it was a phase. I thought she simply didn't know what she wanted. But it stuck. And then all I wanted was for her to find true love, to settle down with someone."

"And she did?"

"Yes. Well, she thought she did, and so did I. She met Aurelie at work. She had a really good job for a local manufacturer. She fell in love with her and I still think Aurelie loved her back. But after ten months of blissful happiness, Aurelie's husband returned from a military operation in Ukraine and Melodie was left with a broken heart."

Ana heard herself gasp in shock. "Oh my god. Did she know Aurelie was married?"

Yvonne shook her head. "She never mentioned it. They spent most of their time together at Melodie's apartment, but she never questioned it since her place was closer to work. It made sense."

Ana's throat tightened. "That's terrible."

"It is. And then she had to quit her job. Aurelie was the owner's niece so she wasn't going anywhere, and Melodie couldn't keep seeing her every day."

"I can imagine." Ana felt deep compassion for Melodie as she tried to envision the pain Aurelie's betrayal might have caused. And a new admiration for her strength. "When did that happen?"

"About two years ago. A couple of months before she hooked up with Kevin. Not a coincidence, if you ask me. Kevin was her high school sweetheart and probably gave her some weird sense of security. Not that she would admit to that, of course."

"What a sad story."

"Oh yes. Thank god we got Thomas out of that mess. I think he saved her in some way. But I still want nothing more than for my granddaughter to find love. Like I found my Raymond. Everyone should have that. And that includes you, dear."

"To be honest, love is not really something I think about. My job takes too much of my time, for one thing, but relationships are also scary. As much as we try, we can never adequately calculate the risks and I'm not a gambler."

Yvonne snorted a laugh. "Nice try. Spoken like a true scientist. But don't forget I know better now. You know how to listen to your gut when it matters. You're here, aren't you? Someday the same pull you felt to this place will push you toward a woman. You'll see. I only hope you find the courage to listen to that gut feeling the same way you listened to the one that brought you here."

Ana threw the ball a little farther than she'd intended. She was disturbed by Yvonne's words. This place, that woman, everything suddenly seemed strangely linked together and she had to force those silly thoughts out of her mind. They started to sound like something close to fate and she didn't believe in fate. She hadn't been led here by some mysterious force. She was here for science. She had a job to do. "Do you mind if we cut our walk a little short today? I need to get ready for my meeting."

CHAPTER FOURTEEN

Ana came back from her meeting in the late afternoon. She'd learned so much. She could have listened to Professor Hubert talk for a few more hours but she'd respected the time he'd allotted her. He'd already been so generous. They'd discussed climate change and rising seas, of course, but also other ways men had contributed to shoreline erosion in the area. He'd explained that in the past, people had collected sand from the beach for construction or other purposes in such large quantities that they reduced the beach's natural capacity to absorb waves. He'd also mentioned people's obsession with building by the water, weakening the beach. In other words, people were destroying the natural layer of protection that was between them and the sea. People who denied climate change often claimed erosion was a natural phenomenon man couldn't control, and it was true. Part of erosion was natural, but man had severely accelerated that natural process with their behaviors. And in both directions. Not only had they developed a dependency on fossil fuels that caused climate change and sea levels to rise, but they'd also managed to weaken the shoreline that was there to protect them. Double whammy. Way to go, people.

She climbed the stairs to the front door of the White Sheep Inn with the intention to run to her room and turn on her laptop so she could type up the ideas that twirled through her mind. She quickly understood as she opened the door, however, that her ideas would have to remain locked inside her brain a little while longer.

Melodie was holding the phone to one ear as she plugged in the other with her finger and Thomas was screaming to the top of his lungs from his bassinet. Ana saw the distress on Melodie's face and knew she had to help. She quickly took off her boots and let her backpack fall to the ground before she ran to the bassinet and took him in her arms. She hurried to the kitchen where his screams wouldn't disturb Melodie. She was ready to look for a bottle to feed him when he calmed down, apparently satisfied simply being held. She looked at him and when he smiled she relaxed. She used her thumb to dry the tears on his round cheeks and he stared at her with these big blue eyes. "You missed me, huh?" He giggled as if to answer, and she realized she'd definitely missed him.

She put him down on the counter just long enough to take off her winter jacket and hold him more comfortably. With a happy baby in her arms, she took her jacket to hang it on the stairway's balusters to make sure she wouldn't forget it downstairs and winked at Melodie, who was still on the phone, standing behind the reception desk. Melodie smiled her gratitude, and Ana felt a familiar fluttering in her stomach. She wanted to hate the sensation and reject it, but she stood defenceless, holding a boy she was unexplainably getting attached to and unable to look away from a woman who terrified and captivated her at the same time.

"Great, we'll have your room ready on December thirty-first, Mr. Smith. Have a lovely day." Melodie hung up the phone and kept observing the interaction between Ana and Thomas.

She was sitting at her usual table in the dining room with Thomas in her arms, their gazes locked on one another.

The tenderness she saw in the woman she'd qualified as rigid a couple of days earlier moved her the same way it had the first time she'd seen her cradle Thomas. Perhaps it was because she'd never seen him so peaceful in anyone's arms besides her grandmother's or her own when she wasn't an anxious mess. It was as if he recognized something in Ana. Her strength, probably. No, her calm. Or her assurance. Qualities she lacked and admired in Ana. But she couldn't admire her, she reminded herself. It was too dangerous. So as much as she hated breaking the magic, she did. "Thank you so much. You saved me," she declared as she stepped around the reception desk and walked to the dining room.

Ana turned to her and smiled. "It wasn't a problem at all. I like spending time with this little guy."

Melodie got close enough to notice the sincere affection in Ana's green eyes. Like her smile, they communicated warmth and endearment, and although the sentiment was addressed to her son, Melodie was deeply touched by it. "Well, I appreciate your help anyway. That man called to make a reservation, but he kept asking questions about the area, the weather, what there was to do in the winter. It was the longest call ever. Do I look like a tour guide to you?"

Ana laughed a low, breathy laughter that broke another piece of that so-called rigidity Melodie had seen in her. She smiled, torn between two opposite needs. On one hand, she wished for Ana's stern character to come back at last so she could feel safe again, but on the other hand, she simply wanted to make her laugh longer. "Where is Yvonne?" Ana asked, breaking the spell.

"She took the afternoon off to do some Christmas shopping with a friend of hers. Here, let me have him. I'm sure you have better things to do."

She took Thomas from Ana's arms before she had a chance to protest. She appeared lost and empty sitting alone on the wooden chair for a few seconds before she caught up with what was happening and answered. "Okay. Well, I guess I'll go type up a few notes before I head out again for dinner."

Melodie watched her gather her boots, backpack, and winter jacket. She turned to the window to see that the light afternoon snow had intensified, and she figured she owed her at least a meal for the way she'd taken care of Thomas. A meal would be safe enough, right? "Anais," she called.

"Yes?"

"I was planning on making carbonara. There'll be plenty for two if you want to join me. It's kind of getting nasty out there. You shouldn't drive in that mess unless you have to."

"Sure. I love carbonara. And if yours is as good as your eggs Benedict I'd be crazy to say no." Her smile was back and she seemed genuinely excited by the invitation.

"Great. It'll be ready in about an hour. Maybe we can have that chat about the article I gave you."

"That sounds perfect. I'll be there. But could you please do me a favor?"

"Maybe, it depends what it is," Melodie answered cautiously. Wasn't cooking for her enough of a favor already?

"Could you please stop calling me Anais? I really, really, really prefer Ana."

Melodie laughed louder than she intended and startled Thomas. "I guess I could do that. I was insisting on calling you Anais to aggravate you but I think we're past that now."

Ana joined in her laughter. "You never sugarcoat things, do you?"

"Only cookies. Maybe I'll make those for you some day. They're delicious. But don't expect me to sugarcoat anything else, no."

"I won't. I think I'm starting to like that about you, actually. It's refreshing. It just takes some getting used to."

"Honesty is very important to me, that's all."

"I understand."

Melodie knew she couldn't possibly understand all the reasons why honesty had become so important to her, from her mother's departure to Aurelie's betrayal. Yet something in the way she said those words, in her compassionate expression, convinced her that she did understand. "Well, I'll see you in an hour. Thank you very much for the invitation, Melodie."

"You're welcome, Ana."

She nodded with satisfaction before she turned and climbed the rest of the stairs. Melodie took Thomas to the kitchen where she prepared a bottle. She wasn't so sure a meal was safe anymore, but she had to admit she couldn't wait to share pasta with Ana. Although being honest with herself remained the most difficult part of honesty. She couldn't even lie to herself about wanting to spend more time with the tousled-haired scientist.

CHAPTER FIFTEEN

Ana came back downstairs as Melodie was setting her table for two. *A* table, she corrected herself. She'd sat at that table for four mornings but it didn't make it hers, did it? She looked around for Thomas and found he was sleeping in the bassinet. Melodie finished placing the silverware on the white tablecloth before she noticed Ana at the bottom of the stairs.

"Now you'll know I eat at your table every night," she explained with a chuckle. "It's the perfect place to keep an eye on Thomas while I have dinner. I hope you don't mind sharing." She chuckled and winked wickedly and Ana felt her face heat up, embarrassed.

Yes, she was a creature of habit. She enjoyed discipline and routine. She wasn't ashamed of it, but she didn't appreciate being teased about it. "It's not my table," she objected. "This is your hotel so you can eat wherever you want." She cleared her throat and turned back to Thomas to change the subject. "Does he always sleep through your dinner time?"

"I wish. No, he doesn't. When he's awake, I put his car seat on the table, give him a few toys, and keep him entertained the best I can while I eat. We don't have enough space for a table in our room, and I prefer eating my meals at a proper table whenever possible."

Ana tried to imagine Melodie eating alone at this table every night and for the first time since they'd met, she thought that perhaps her life, as hectic as it was with the inn and a child to take care of, could at times leave her as lonely as Ana was. "Understandable," she acknowledged. "Can I help with anything?"

"No, everything is ready. Sit down and I'll go get our plates. You can serve the wine if you want." Ana glanced at the Chablis on the table. "Please tell me you drink wine. I never drink but I like a good wine once in a while when I have company, which I'm sure you can imagine is rare with a six-month-old baby."

Ana wasn't really fond of wine or alcohol in general, but fortunately she could tolerate white wine, sometimes even appreciate it. "Chablis sounds perfect with carbonara, actually. It smells divine, by the way."

"Wonderful. Go ahead and pour us two glasses and I'll be right back with the food."

Ana watched Melodie walk to the kitchen and realized she'd changed into a crocheted V-neck sweater and jeans. The look was still casual but a little more daring than the T-shirt she'd worn earlier. The jeans beautifully hugged her hips and showcased her round butt. Although the loose fit of the sweater hid her curves, the crochet allowed a glimpse of a black bra. Ana closed her eyes and took a deep breath before she poured the wine.

She could not remember the last time she'd looked at a woman this way. The last time she'd noticed clothes, curves, skin or any other physical attribute that had made her own body burn. Melodie had left her cold as well at one point. It was as if her body followed her lead. The more she learned to appreciate Melodie for the amazing qualities that had been buried under her bad attitude when they'd first met, the more she noticed her physical attributes. Cause and effect. Oh, who was she kidding? There was nothing scientific about what was going on.

Melodie took her time to serve two generous portions of spaghetti Carbonara in pasta dishes. She needed to regain her composure before she went back to the dining room. She'd come too close to running her hand through Ana's unruly auburn mane. She'd come too close to caressing the sleeve of her green and black striped cashmere sweater. That green made her eyes pop up like two emeralds. It wasn't fair. She had to know that particular sweater had that effect on her eyes. She had to know it made her damn nearly irresistible. It wasn't fair. And it wouldn't work. She grabbed the plates and headed out of the kitchen, determined. She caught Ana's longing gaze on her as she approached the table and realized her own choice of clothes might not have been that innocent either.

"Voilà. Carbonara for two. I hope you like it," she announced as she placed it in front of Ana.

"If it tastes as good as it smells, I'll love it."

Melodie took a sip of wine and let it coat her mouth, savoring it as she watched Ana take her first bite of pasta. She waited anxiously for her reaction and swallowed her wine when Ana hummed her appreciation. She relished the lemon quality and tingling sensation of the Chablis mixed with the pride she always took in watching someone enjoy her cooking. Ana's pleasure was unrestrained and filled her with so much joy she caught herself giggling.

"This is the best carbonara I've ever had. Seriously. I think you're spoiling me."

"It's the pasta water."

"What?"

"A lot of people put cream in their carbonara sauce but there's no cream in an authentic carbonara. The creaminess comes from the mix of eggs and pasta water."

"That's fascinating, but I'm sure that's not the only thing that makes this so good."

"Well, I can't tell you all of my secrets, can I?"

"Of course not. That said, your secrets would be safe with me. You could give me the entire secret recipe and I guarantee I couldn't reproduce it. I'm worthless in a kitchen."

"That's strange. It's a little like science after all. You measure ingredients, mix them together."

"That's baking. I can bake. Baking is an exact science. This, however, is something else." She continued twisting her fork into the pasta. "This comes from the heart."

"You might be right about that," Melodie replied as she watched Ana savor another bite. "A few days ago I might have said that's why you can't cook, then," she added teasingly before she took a bite of her own pasta.

Ana furrowed her brows in puzzlement before she seemed to understand the joke. "Oh, right. Because I'm rigid and I don't have a heart. Very funny."

Melodie laughed as Ana pointed her fork at her and narrowed her eyes to pretend she was offended. "I think it's very funny. That said, I know better now. You have a heart, Ana Bloom. It's obvious when you hold Thomas. And when you eat my food."

"Oh no, I guess I've been caught. You've uncovered my darkest secret," she said as she shoved a large amount of pasta into her mouth and chewed eagerly.

Melodie laughed again, pleased to find out that Ana not only had a heart, but a sense of humor as well. She wanted to find out more about her. "Tell me about your life in the States. Do you live in a large city?"

Ana swallowed before she answered. "No, Ithaca is larger than Sainte-Luce-Sur-Mer, of course, but it's pretty small. It's mostly a college town."

"Does your family live there too?"

"I don't have any family left, as a matter of fact." The answer was given dryly, between two bites. Ana didn't even look at her, and she knew she shouldn't pry, but she couldn't help digging a little more.

"Really? No brother or sister? No parents? No one at all?"

Ana looked at her this time. She recognized sadness in her eyes, and perhaps anger. "No one. I never knew my father. Never had brothers or sisters. And my mother died last month."

"I'm sorry," she whispered before she rested her hand on Ana's to comfort her. She should have minded her own business, but she was used to stepping over the line and apologizing for it afterward. "Was she ill?"

"Cancer."

"That's terrible."

"It is, but it's not like we were close. My mother wasn't exactly the maternal type. Our relationship was polite at best and nonexistent for long periods of time. When she told me she had cancer, I took her in out of obligation. I came here right after her funeral. Some might say I was running away, but I prefer thinking I had to move on and keep busy." Ana's tone was dry, guarded, but Melodie caught tears filling her eyes before Ana closed them and squared her jaw. Ana obviously had unfinished business with her mother despite her death and Melodie was dying to dig deeper and find out why, but probing would leave her open to be probed and she wasn't ready to open up to Ana about her own mother.

Melodie noticed she'd been caressing Ana's hand and froze, hesitating for a few seconds before she resumed the comforting movement of her fingers. Ana was using her fork to push pasta around her plate. She'd apparently lost her appetite. "You took care of her anyway. That's admirable. I'm not sure I could do that for my mother." She clicked her tongued, regretting her words as soon as they came out.

"Why? Don't you get along with your mother?"

She scoffed. "No. Our relationship is nonexistent, as you put it. She left when I was fourteen and I saw her once or twice a year after that until I was eighteen. I've seen her three times since then. She hasn't even met Thomas yet. She wanted a big career in Montreal. She wanted to get away from here. From us."

"Us?"

"Me and my dad." She left Ana's hand alone on the table to wipe tears from her eyes. "But please don't talk about this with my grandmother. She still thinks my mother asked me to move in with her and I'm the one who decided not to go."

"But she didn't?" She shook her head. "Would you have gone?"

She shrugged. "Probably not. I don't know." She ran her hands through her curls and massaged her scalp as she took a deep breath, attempting to chase those dark thoughts away. When she grabbed her glass of wine and rested her other hand back on the table, Ana covered it in the same manner she'd covered hers earlier.

"I guess that's one thing we have in common. Complicated relationships with our mothers." Melodie nodded as she focused on the pressure of Ana's warm hands on hers. "At least you have Yvonne. And Thomas." Ana lowered her eyes and swallowed and Melodie understood that Ana had it even worse for she was completely alone in the world. And from the way she'd talked about her mother, perhaps she'd been alone all her life.

"Yes, I'm very lucky." Ana smiled and slowly dragged her hand away, leaving her with one last caress, a soft but firm stroke that she felt on her skin long after Ana's hand got back to holding her fork and took another bite. She still didn't look like she had much of an appetite, but she was eating, and Melodie decided to steer the conversation to less personal matters. "So what did you think of that article? Good stuff, huh?"

"Yes, very interesting."

"So, do you still think moving away from the shore is the best option?"

"Yes, I'm afraid so."

"What?"

Ana swallowed with difficulty. A few minutes earlier she would have preferred any topic of conversation over her mother. She'd been forced to think of Constance again and to stir deeply rooted anger and resentment. She preferred keeping those feelings buried inside her, but the longer she stayed at the White Sheep Inn and the more time she spent with Yvonne, Melodie, and Thomas, the more difficult it became to keep them from flaring up and tormenting her. It was extremely unpleasant, yet it was better than the confrontation that was about to take place.

At least they'd connected as they talked about their respective relationships with their mothers. Ana felt vulnerable right now, not in the right state of mind to argue her convictions at all, but she didn't have a choice.

"Don't get me wrong. There are wonderful ideas in the article you gave me. A few years ago I would probably have defended them with you. I'm an engineering geologist, after all. We live for these types of ideas. The guy who suggested adding turbines to a protective wall to generate green energy is brilliant. But that's not the way I think anymore."

Melodie's features hardened as she spoke. "No, you're making that crystal clear. You prefer giving up. What kind of scientist are you?" She didn't look at Ana as she made the biting accusation. She focused on her plate, plunging her fork into her pasta repeatedly as if she were stabbing it.

Ana reached over the table to grab her wrist, gently but firmly, forcing her to meet her gaze. "I'm not giving up, Melodie. I'm just choosing a different strategy. I'm the kind of scientist who doesn't think the solution to fixing the way we messed with nature is to mess with it even more. There are more and more like me, fortunately. And if scientists had always thought a little bit more like we do, we wouldn't be in this much trouble now."

"So you cross your arms and observe as the sea destroys everything we own? That's your solution?"

"No, not at all. I help people organize, find assistance from governments and businesses, come up with a plan and priorities, and do the only sensible thing to do: relocate. Then I find ways everyone can keep enjoying the beach without endangering or weakening it even more, maybe even go as far as planting sea grass to help strengthen it again, but mainly try to stay away from it. It might not be as exciting as building fancy walls, but it's what I truly believe is the best thing to do."

Melodie scoffed and jerked her arm out of her grasp. "You've never lived by the sea, have you?"

"No."

"Of course not. If you had, you'd understand that people who grow up by the sea can't simply move away. It's part of who we are. We have saltwater running through our veins. Don't you get it? You can't expect us to abandon our homes because you think it's the best thing to do. Who are you to decide what's the best thing to do anyway?"

"So you'd rather build a gigantic wall in the sea you love so much than learn to appreciate it from a distance?"

"You don't understand. It's simply not an option for us. We have to stay. And walls don't have to be as invasive as you make them sound. What about the MOSE project in Venice?"

"You mean the huge mobile gates that will cost billions to build and will be useless once they're finished because the sea levels will already have surpassed the engineers' predictions?" She recognized sarcasm in her own tone and took a deep breath to calm down. She wouldn't achieve anything if she became as defensive as Melodie, who was now leaning away from the table against the back of her chair, her arms crossed on her chest. "Look, all I'm saying is that I may not have grown up by the sea, but I have nothing but respect for it. I respect its power, and I'd rather spend my time and energy helping people learn to respect it rather than fight against it, try to change it or tame it in any way."

"Maybe I was wrong. Maybe you don't have a heart after all," Melodie said through clenched teeth.

"Excuse me?"

"It's easy for you to sit there and talk about respect and appreciating the sea from a distance. You've never loved anything in your whole life. If you had you'd know that you can't love from a distance, Ana. You may respect the sea, as you say, but we love it. Love is stronger than your fucking respect and you can't reason with it. If you knew anything about love you'd do everything you can to help us stay. But all you know about is running away, so you expect us to do the same."

Ana swallowed and closed her eyes to chase away threatening tears. Maybe she could have accepted Melodie's rant if their earlier conversation hadn't left her emotions so raw and vulnerable. Maybe she could have taken it less personally if she hadn't been reminded once again that the only person who should have loved her unconditionally since her birth had never been able to do so. Maybe she could have shrugged it off if it hadn't been right. Ana didn't know anything about love. If Melodie wanted to hurt her, she'd succeeded, and she was done protecting her feelings. "Love won't do anything for you when a storm wipes out this precious inn of yours," she said coldly. "Thank you for dinner, but I think I'll go to my room now," she added before she got up and walked to the stairs.

"That's right. Run, Anais. That's what you do best."

She dug her fingers into the wooden railing of the stairway and clenched her jaw. She was tempted to turn around and fight back, but she didn't know what to say. There was nothing more to say. Melodie wouldn't listen. She would attack. And she'd been hurt enough for one night. She climbed the stairs without looking back and found refuge in her room. She stared at the notes she'd been typing about her meeting with Professor Hubert, unable to focus.

Melodie cried as she did the dishes and cried again as she played with Thomas once they got back to their room, sitting on the foam mat. She knew she'd been hurtful, but she didn't regret it. She'd been hurtful on purpose, at least. Ana was cruel without even realizing it. She truly believed there was nothing wrong with asking people who'd lived by the sea all their lives to simply move away. Even worse, she had the knowledge and resources to help them fight against the threat of rising sea levels and consciously chose not to. Because she didn't think it was the right thing to do. Because it went against her convictions. Well, screw her convictions. Screw her thick auburn hair, green eyes, and soft skin. She was nothing but a selfish know-it-all and Melodie had been an idiot to think there could be a softer, kinder side to her. A side she'd even thought she was attracted to. Screw Anais Bloom.

"Damn shit," she whispered to herself. Thomas answered with loud laughter and she brought her attention back to him. He was holding a textured book she'd read to him every night since his birth. It told the story of a baby whale as he discovered the sea with his mother. It was a sweet story, although Thomas currently seemed more interested in chewing on the soft fabric cover. She picked up the boy and sat him between her legs before she took the book from him so she could read. "Don't worry, my love. You'll grow up by the sea just like we all did," she said as she got lost in the deep blue colors of the illustrated pages.

CHAPTER SIXTEEN

Present

Ana threw the ball again, but closer this time. Miller had obviously lost the stamina he'd gained the year before thanks to their daily walks. He was also a year older, probably about six years old if she remembered well, not too old to get in shape again. "We'll take it easy, old man," she said as she rubbed his head when he brought back the ball.

Ana had been at the White Sheep Inn for three days and Melodie still refused to have a conversation with her. She answered no more than yes or no to her questions when she answered at all. She never smiled at her like she did with other guests. Never laughed with her about trivial things like she did with them. Yet Ana found hope in the fact that she let her stay at the inn. She could have said there was no vacancy. Ana would have known it wasn't true in the middle of December, but it would have sent a clear message. Instead she'd given her room number one. Ana had been inexplicably happy holding the red plastic key chain and its fading number one again.

Melodie served her breakfast every morning and changed her towels every day. She even let her hold and play with Thomas, and she let her take Miller for long walks. These were all reasons to hope, but Ana knew she would have to be patient. Melodie was as stubborn as they came, and the only way Ana would get her to listen was if she was just as stubborn. "I'm not running. Not this time," she declared to a panting Miller. She crouched down to give him some water from the special bottle she'd bought for him the year before. "Let's go back home. I have an idea."

She walked into the lobby and saw Melodie play with Thomas behind the reception desk. She was tickling the boy, whose laughter was so joyful Ana had to smile. Melodie ignored her as usual. Miller sprawled out on the floor by the desk, exhausted. She climbed the stairs and went to her room, where she took off her boots and jacket and rummaged through her backpack until she found the article she was looking for. She used her hand to smooth over a corner of the title page that had flared up and read the title with pride, "Living on the Edge."

She went back downstairs where Melodie and Thomas were still playing. She approached the desk knowing Melodie would keep ignoring her, placed the article on the desk, and walked back to the stairs.

"What's that?" she heard Melodie ask.

She turned to answer. "It's the article I wrote about Sainte-Luce-Sur-Mer. It got published. I thought you might like to read it."

Melodie put Thomas in his playpen and turned to her at last. Her narrowed, light blue gaze sent a cold current through Ana's veins. "Oh, Anais. Of all people, you should really know better than to waste paper like this. Where's your ecological consciousness? I have no interest in reading this article and you know it."

"Well, I think you should."

"I don't care what you think I should do." Her tone was as glacial as her stare and Ana felt her airways tighten. She opened her mouth to speak but decided any argument would be fruitless while Melodie remained so closed off. She turned to go back upstairs, surprised when Melodie added, "You never answered me."

"Excuse me?" she asked as she dared to meet her gaze again.

"When you arrived, I asked you what you were doing here. You never answered me."

Ana stepped closer, until the only thing that stood between them was the reception desk. She held her gaze, knowing the answer had to be crystal clear in her own eyes, hoping she could see it. "I think you know what I'm doing here."

Melodie averted her eyes and pointed at the window. "No, I really don't. Didn't you see the frozen sea out there? What happened last year won't happen again. There's nothing for you to study."

"I'm not here about what happened that night and you know it. Look at me." She did, and Ana saw that the icy stare was starting to break. "I'm here about what happened after that. Everything that led to…that other night," she added with difficulty.

Melodie's eyes welled up with tears and she turned her back to Ana. "What happened that night won't happen again either. So you might as well leave now."

"Melodie," she started.

"No," she blurted out as she faced her again, her frigid expression back in full force. "Leave me alone."

Ana nodded and went back to her room where she cried quietly, trying to hang on to her hope. Her article had remained on the reception desk. Maybe she would read it later. If she did, she would understand.

CHAPTER SEVENTEEN

One year earlier

"Would you please tell me what happened between the two of you? I thought you were finally learning to get along. Then I take off for one afternoon and when I get back the next morning, you can't even look at each other. Ana seems very upset. What did you do to her?"

Melodie topped off the yogurt parfait with granola while Yvonne went on and on behind her in the kitchen. Of course it had to be her fault. Her grandmother couldn't take her side against Ana, could she? So what was the point in trying to explain? She turned around and handed her the breakfast plate. "I really don't want to get into this with you, Mammie. Can you please just take her damn yogurt?"

Yvonne took the plate and sighed with frustration before she left the kitchen. Melodie started cleaning, hoping her grandmother wouldn't return, but she knew better. She wouldn't leave it alone. She was back before Melodie could finish putting away the three ingredients she'd needed to make Ana's breakfast. Yvonne stood in the middle of the room, her hands on her hips, staring at her as she wiped the counter with a dishcloth.

She wouldn't escape her grandmother. She never could. Her best option was to make her understand she wouldn't back down. She rubbed the countertop harder as she talked, "You're right. We were starting to get along. When she offered to take care of Thomas so I could take you to the doctor, I even thought you were right about her so-called kindness. I went as far as inviting her to share dinner with me last night."

"That's good."

"No Mammie. It wasn't good." She dropped the dishcloth on the countertop and turned to face her grandmother. "That dinner made me see the real Ana, the one who thinks she knows what's best for us and won't back down from her own fucking beliefs, even for one minute to try to understand what we really need. She could help us, you know."

"That's what she's trying to do, dear," Yvonne said to appease her as she caressed her face.

"No, what she's trying to do is prove a point. Her damn theory. She could really help us fight against this, but all she wants is to convince us we should give up. Why do you think she's chosen this place? Because there's a handful of us and she thinks we're gullible enough to listen. Anywhere else people would laugh at her and tell her to fuck off."

"Melodie—"

"No. Don't even try to say she's right. I'm telling you this because you insisted and now you know what happened. And I need you to understand once and for all that I will never think the way she does. You think what you want, but I will never agree with her. She will never convince me leaving this place is the right thing to do. Can you please respect that? That's all I'm asking. I will cook for her. I will wash her dirty towels and her sheets. I will do what I would do for any other guest while she's here, but don't ask me to make nice again. It won't happen. Is that clear?"

Yvonne simply nodded with a sigh of defeat and Melodie walked past her to exit the kitchen. She felt Ana's eyes on her as she walked through the dining room but she avoided her gaze. She went straight to the bassinet where Thomas was... not. She turned and found him sitting peacefully in Ana's lap, chewing on his giraffe while Ana ate her breakfast. She felt her blood turn to a boil instantly.

"What do you think you're doing?" she barked as she rushed to Ana's table.

"He started to cry, so I comforted him. That's all."

"Well, from now on I'll be the one comforting my son, you got that?" she said as calmly as she could not to upset Thomas as she took him from Ana's lap.

"Got it. I was trying to help."

"We don't need your help. Please don't touch my son again." She took him toward their room and turned around at the stairway to add, "Have a good day, Ms. Bloom." She noticed Ana's eyes were swollen and bloodshot, but she hurried to her room before empathy had a chance to mix with her anger. She wouldn't let Ana weaken her resolve again. Ever.

"I tried, Yvonne. I did my best to explain my beliefs, but she seems to think I have some kind of evil agenda. Like all I want is to tear people away from their beloved sea. Everything I said only made her hate me even more. And then she said things I won't repeat but she really hurt me. I can't go through this again. I'm sorry."

"No, I'm the one who owes you an apology. I shouldn't have insisted so much. I can only imagine the horrible things she said to you. She can be awful when she gets defensive. I thought she could understand the logic behind relocating, but obviously I was wrong."

She felt Yvonne's hand rub her back as they stood side by side, facing the sea. She breathed in the strong salty winds and watched Miller sniff around rocks and driftwood in the sand. There was no snow left on the ground, no ice on the water as far as she could see. Only raging waves crashing on the beach. They seemed threatening even at low tide. It was unsafe to take a walk during high tides. And they would keep getting worse until they reached solstice heights in three days. Ana only hoped the low-pressure system shown moving their way would unexpectedly change its trajectory or weaken. "If the storm that's supposed to hit us this weekend is bad, she'll probably blame me for that too."

Yvonne snorted a laugh and bumped her arm with her shoulder. "She did say you were just trying to prove a point. A storm would be a grand way to do it."

Ana glanced at Yvonne and saw her wink. She smiled but was unable to find as much humor in the situation as the older woman did. She turned back to the sea with a sigh. "If she only knew how much I wished we would've stopped abusing the planet before we reached this point. What I would do to turn back time and avoid all this."

Yvonne put her arm around her and squeezed reassuringly, pressing her to her side as they both kept observing the waves. "I know, dear. I know."

Miller whined at her feet and she looked down. "You're right, buddy. Let's walk. Shall we?" she added as she turned to Yvonne.

"Absolutely. Enough brooding already."

Ana reached into her jacket pocket for the blue ball and threw it for the dog as they walked west on the beach. They walked in silence for a few minutes before Yvonne added, "At least Thomas will be staying with his dad this weekend. They live in the boonies but he'll be safe there. I'll be okay at the duplex too, but I'm sure Melodie will refuse to leave the inn."

Ana looked at Yvonne and understood the silent request in her soft, worried blue eyes. She took her hand. "Don't worry. I'll watch over her."

Yvonne squeezed her hand in response. "I don't doubt it."

CHAPTER EIGHTEEN

Kevin had already packed the bassinet, toys, and everything else that needed to follow a six-month-old on any overnight trip. Melodie had called him the night before to say that his pickup truck wouldn't do but was pleasantly surprised when he'd answered he'd already asked to borrow his parents' SUV. Maybe he wasn't completely hopeless after all. But the thought didn't keep her from making sure the car seat was installed properly before she let him leave with Thomas. Just in case. After a thorough inspection, she turned to Kevin, who stood by the car with Thomas in his arms and a grin on his face. "Did I pass?"

"I must admit I'm impressed."

"So will you let us leave now? They're waiting for us to have breakfast."

"You're free to go. But don't hesitate to call if you have any questions at all."

"Relax, Mel. I'll be in a house full of people who raised or are raising children of their own. They won't let me fuck up even if I wanted to."

"I guess you have a point there," she replied with a chuckle. "All right, let me get him in his seat and then I'll let you go." She took Thomas from his arms and was pleased when Kevin stayed behind her to observe as she secured Thomas. These things could be tricky. She kissed Thomas on the nose and closed the door, trying to fight against the tightening in her heart. "You drive carefully now," she warned Kevin as he walked around to the driver's door.

"Promise. Seriously, Mel, I swear nothing bad will happen. Okay?" She simply nodded. "We'll be back tomorrow afternoon. Enjoy your weekend. Do something special. Go out with your friends or have one of those long baths with candles and those disgustingly sweet smells you like so much."

She let out a loud laugh that temporarily relaxed her tension, releasing some of the tears that she'd kept at bay until then. She wiped them away as she kept laughing. "That's not a bad idea, actually."

"I do have good ideas once in a while, you know." He winked at her and got behind the wheel of the car that looked entirely too grown-up for him. She watched them leave and couldn't help but feel empty. Fortunately she didn't have time to stand there and wallow in self-pity. She glanced at her watch. Seven fifteen. Ana would be waiting for her breakfast. She hurried inside, left her boots and jacket behind the reception desk, put on her comfortable shoes and went straight to the kitchen. All without a single glance in Ana's direction.

Once in the kitchen she found her grandmother lining up ingredients for eggs Benedict. "Where's the Hollandaise sauce?"

"Let me," she said as she took Yvonne's place in front of the fridge and reached for a plastic container. "I made a fresh batch last night."

"Really? How did you know? She's had yogurt all week."

"All week except last Saturday. She said she has eggs Benedict once a week, so I knew she'd order them today. I guess being boring and predictable has its perks. I've got this, Mammie. Go get her more coffee. It's time for her second cup."

"Why must you be so mean?"

"If I were that mean I'd dump hot sauce all over her eggs. Don't tempt me. I think I'm doing a really great job at controlling my urges."

Yvonne shook her head, holding a fresh pot of coffee. "You're impossible. You know that?"

"How could I forget?" Yvonne left the kitchen and she focused on the delicate orchestration making eggs Benedict represented. She wouldn't sabotage Ana's breakfast, of course. The bitch wasn't worth ruining a recipe she'd spent years perfecting.

Ana savored her eggs with pure pleasure. She'd been waiting all week to indulge in Melodie's recipe again, expecting that she might have exaggerated how delicious they tasted and would be disappointed on her second try. She'd been wrong. If anything, they tasted even better this morning. Yet as good as they were, she couldn't enjoy them in peace. In fact, her delightful breakfast was being disturbed on two fronts, the first being the whirlwind of thoughts in her own mind. She'd followed the progress of the storm on her laptop and unless things changed unexpectedly, it would pass over their heads around the same time as this evening's high tide, predicted to be close to sixteen feet high. The combination of both events could be catastrophic.

Her second source of distraction came from the kitchen, where Melodie's and Yvonne's voices grew louder. Melodie finally stormed out of the kitchen yelling something in French. She already knew they were arguing about Melodie going to stay with her grandmother in her duplex for the night because Yvonne had mentioned it to her earlier. Apparently it was going as well as she'd expected.

"*T'es pas raisonnable,*" Yvonne argued behind her. She then turned to Ana and shook her head before she continued in English, probably hoping for help in convincing her granddaughter. "Listen to the radio. They say it could be worse than 2010. I have a guest room ready for you. I'd feel so much better knowing you're safe with me."

They made their way behind the reception desk before Melodie continued, "I'm not going anywhere."

Ana agreed that Melodie being safe with Yvonne during the storm was a much better idea than staying here. She hesitated before she spoke, knowing Melodie probably wouldn't react well to her butting in, but in the end she chose to show her support to Yvonne. "Your grandmother is right. You'll be safer in the village. And don't worry about me. I'll be all right by myself."

"I'm not staying for you," she hissed with all her venom. "I'm not going to be chased away by any scientist or any storm, you hear me?" She disappeared into the hall behind the stairway and Ana heard a door slam a few seconds later.

"I'm sorry," she told Yvonne, who joined her in the dining room and sat across from her at the table. "I was trying to help but I might have made things worse instead."

Yvonne waved her hand dismissively. "Don't worry. I could never have convinced her anyway. Sorry we disturbed your breakfast."

"Oh it's okay. Don't worry about it." She took a bite and looked at Miller, who'd stared at her through the entire episode. "With everything going on today, I think he's the only one who could still focus on breakfast."

Yvonne chuckled briefly. "I'll feed him in a minute, but then I think we'll head up to the village. There's no sense trying to go for a walk today."

"You're right."

"You're a good person, Ana. We've only known each other for a week but I already consider you a friend."

"So do I," Ana replied as she met Yvonne's gaze, heavy with concern.

"And as a friend, I should invite you to come with me today, but I can't. Instead of helping my friend, I need to ask her for a favor."

Ana placed her hand on Yvonne's arm, trembling as it rested on the table. "I promised you I'd watch over her, and I will. Besides, I need to stay here, in the middle of the action."

"Thank you."

Ana smiled at her before she stood and grabbed her plate. "Now you go feed Miller and get out of here. I'll clean the kitchen. And don't worry. If I think we're not safe here, I'll drag her out one way or another. I'll carry her over my shoulder like a sack of potatoes and I'll find a way to bring her to you."

Yvonne snorted a laugh. "That would be a sight. If it comes to that, be aware that your sack of potatoes will be kicking, biting, scratching, and screaming louder than any sack of potatoes you've ever met."

They both laughed and Yvonne surprised her when she stood and hugged her tightly before she thanked her again. Ana returned the embrace, slowly growing used to Yvonne's spontaneous warmth and affection. She would do anything for her, even watch over a woman who couldn't stand her presence.

CHAPTER NINETEEN

Ana decided she'd stay outside as long as she could. She didn't want to put her own security at risk, but she felt it was her duty to experience the storm she'd feared and predicted. It had all been theories until now. She wanted to see it, breathe it, feel it for as long as she could stand it. It wouldn't be much longer. She was already terrified. No one knew how bad things would get yet, but there was no doubt it would get bad. Ana stood on the beach behind the inn, keeping her promise to Yvonne to watch over Melodie. That woman was so infuriating. She should be in the village with her grandmother. She had no business staying so close to the storm. Ana knew she was stubbornly trying to prove a point, which made Ana feel even more responsible for her safety.

She faced the sea and couldn't remember ever feeling so small. The tide was rising. It wouldn't get to its highest point for another hour or so, yet it was already menacing. Strong winds coming from the north hit the sea at fifty miles per hour, building waves up before they crashed onto rocks or on the beach with such force that the impact resembled explosions of water, spraying everything several feet around them. Winds were predicted to strengthen as the water rose, unleashing its power. It was only a matter of time before waves crashed against houses. They'd probably reach the inn. She shuddered, the humid air penetrating through her raincoat to her skin, to her bones. Or was she shuddering out of fear? Probably both.

She knew what was happening, how and why it was happening, but she also knew she couldn't possibly guess where it would stop and how much damage it would cause. She felt completely powerless as she breathed with difficulty through the thick, heavy, salty mist. She cupped her hands over her ears, trying to muffle the deafening sounds she couldn't even identify anymore. Wind and waves became a single rumbling, as if a train was about to run over her. She spotted a red plastic Adirondack chair in the water not too far from where she was standing. The sea rocked it back and forth. The sight almost comforted her until she saw the chair disappear into a wave. She turned and saw the beach behind her was no longer dry and she stood in water. The streetlights that had turned on as soon as the sun had disappeared were off. No light came from the inn either. The winds had probably caused power outages. Her heart thumped hard, giving a beat to the roaring noise around her. It was time to go back in.

She walked toward the inn when one of her Wellington boots got caught in mud and she tripped. As she lay flat on her stomach on the wet ground, a wave passed over her and she felt the sand sink under her body. The water was freezing. If she didn't move quickly she'd be doomed to the same fate as that red plastic chair, swallowed whole by the sea. Panicked, she crawled as fast as she could until she could stand up again and ran to the inn without looking back.

She'd experienced enough of the storm already, but she wasn't convinced the walls of the inn would keep her or Melodie safe. She thought about dragging her to the car and escaping to the village, but she figured the water had probably reached the road to the west and east of their location. It was too late to run. They'd have to face the storm together. Trapped inside and hoping for the best. She took a deep breath and walked into the dark lobby. "Melodie!"

"I'm in here!" a trembling voice yelled back in the direction of the hall. She reached for the flashlight she kept in her backpack and headed toward Melodie's room.

Melodie had decided to indulge in a long sweet-scented bath as Kevin had suggested. It was a luxury she couldn't afford anymore with Thomas constantly demanding her attention, a luxury she'd even forgotten about until Kevin had reminded her that morning. She slowly lit a dozen of candles that she distributed around the ledge of the bathtub and on the vanity as hot water filled the tub and a mandarin-scented steam filled the room. She got in the bath and tried to relax despite winds growing stronger outside. She was used to the sound of wind and waves crashing on the beach. She heard the walls and windows crack a little, but that wasn't new either. There was no reason to run away and her grandmother wouldn't have insisted so much if Ana hadn't been around. Her grandmother had never been scared of a storm before. Ana was frightening her with her alarmist ideas.

Melodie focused on her breathing and the light dancing around her. She'd left the bathroom door slightly open so the bedroom light could come in without flooding the warm candlelight. She'd missed Thomas all day, but she had a feeling Kevin would take him more often moving forward. She'd seen something different in him today. Less of a boy and more of a man. She wanted him to spend time with their son so she had to find ways to make time without Thomas more pleasurable. This bath was exactly the kind of thing she could see herself looking forward to.

The light coming through the door suddenly disappeared and the inn fell in silence. The power was out. Melodie blew out a few candles, thinking they'd be useful later if the outage lasted through the storm. She sank back into her bubble bath and settled into the dead silence of the house. It was a little creepy, but the worst part of it was that she could now hear every sound the boisterous storm made outside. She could hear the sea as it inched closer and closer, waves crashing louder and louder. She could hear the patio furniture being pushed around the porch, hitting the walls of the inn with a banging noise that made her jump every time. As much as she wanted to remain strong and calm, she felt fear take over, and soon she couldn't stand being in the water anymore.

She got out of the bath and dried herself before she covered her body with a thick pink terrycloth robe. She took two lit candles to her bedside table and blew out the rest of them before she lined them up on the nightstand, ready to be used. She sat on her bed and contemplated getting dressed and driving to the village. She didn't need to prove Ana wrong badly enough to spend the night alone in the dark, terrified. She heard the doorbell, indicating that the front door of the inn had been opened, and was shocked at the way she sighed with relief when she heard Ana's voice call her name.

"I'm in here!" she called back, appalled at the fragility she heard in her own voice. She took a candle and walked to the door. As soon as she opened it she recognized the light beam of a flashlight. "Of course you have a flashlight," she said before she could stop herself.

"Are you really going to poke fun at me for being predictable right now?"

"No. Right now I think you're a freaking genius, to tell you the truth. Come in."

She made room for Ana to enter. Water was dripping from her hair, face, raincoat, everywhere. She was covered with mud and shivering with cold. "You have candles, I see. I'm not the only one who was prepared."

"I wish I could say it was planned that way, but believe it or not, I was just treating myself to a bubble bath in candlelight."

"Oh, well," Ana said as she directed her flashlight to Melodie's terrycloth robe, her teeth chattering. "Good timing then. Those candles will come in handy."

"So will the bath. I just got out and it's still warm. Get in the bathroom, get out of these wet clothes and get warm, will you? Last thing we need is for you to become hypothermic. I would run you a fresh bath, but Mammie upgraded the inn to a tankless water heating system a few years back. An electric system. It's great because even with a full house we never run out of hot water as long as there's electricity, but in a power outage we're screwed."

"I'll be okay. I'm inside now. I'll warm up sooner or later."

"Don't argue with me. Unless I gross you out?"

Melodie felt Ana stare at her and saw her blush. "You don't gross me out at all," she said in a low voice that took Melodie by surprise and sent a warm current down her body. She had to clear her throat before she could speak again. "Good. Then get in there right now. I'll find something for you to wear. And take a couple of these," she added as she handed Ana a candle. "We should save the flashlight in case we need to go out of this room." Ana nodded and turned it off before she handed Melodie the flashlight in exchange for a lit candle. She remained immobile so Melodie gently pushed her inside the bathroom. "Hurry now, before the water gets cold," she whispered before she closed the door.

She sat on the floor and leaned against the door. She heard the thud of Ana's backpack and raincoat falling to the floor, followed by fainter sounds until she recognized the distinct splashing and spattering of bathwater. It was difficult to isolate these sounds from the ruckus the storm was making outside, but Melodie made every effort to focus on any sign of Ana's presence on the other side of the door. She was far past trying to prove a point. This storm was clearly stronger than any storm she'd experienced before and she was glad she wouldn't have to face it alone. As frustrating as Ana's beliefs were, she couldn't think of anyone she'd trust more in this situation.

Ana rubbed the mud off her hands and her face as her body temperature slowly came back to normal in the warm bathwater. She noted the same mandarin scent she'd smelled on Melodie when she'd entered the room. The smell suited the brunette much better than it would suit her, she was sure of that. She preferred more subtle perfumes on her own skin. Or none at all. But mandarin was perfect for Melodie's skin. As idiotic and irresponsible as it seemed for anyone to be taking a bath while all hell prepared to break loose outside, Ana was grateful for the warm water now. She was also grateful for the candles and for the fact that the room was not located on the sea side of the inn. They'd probably be safer here than anywhere else in the building.

She got out of the tub and let the water out. "Towels are on the shelf above the toilet. I'll find you something to wear now," she heard Melodie call out from the other side of the door. She must have heard the sound of water running down the drain, Ana thought. She was patiently waiting for her to be done. She was scared, that much was obvious from the way she'd appeared so pleased to see her earlier. At least she wouldn't have to fight to watch over her during the storm, which she'd been prepared to do. Melodie clearly welcomed her presence. For now anyway.

"Thank you." She dried off and wrapped herself in a towel before she opened the bathroom door to take the clothes Melodie handed her.

"Here. The sweatpants might be a little short for you, but they'll be comfortable." She took the dark sweatpants and plain white T-shirt, both neatly folded.

"You know, I could run upstairs to get my own clothes."

"Please don't," Melodie replied as she moved closer and placed a hand on her bare arm. Ana felt her tremble.

"Why not?"

She clicked her tongue, exasperated. "You're going to make me say it, aren't you?"

"Say what?"

"That I'm scared shitless and I don't want to be alone. Happy now?"

Ana couldn't help chuckling briefly, glad Melodie could admit her fear, but she didn't want to torture her either. She squeezed the hand that was still resting on her arm before she met her anxious gaze. "Let me just get into these clothes and we'll get settled for the night. I'm not going anywhere, I promise. We'll be okay."

"How can you be so sure?"

Ana simply smiled and got back inside the bathroom but didn't close the door completely. She couldn't be sure, but what else could she say? They were stuck here now. There was no sense panicking. She hurried into the sweatpants that were indeed at least two inches too short for her. She put on the T-shirt and glanced at the mirror above the vanity. The T-shirt she'd thought plain actually sported a small drawing of a beluga on her chest with the words "*Sauvons les Belugas*" written in blue under it. Save the belugas. Ana smiled. The small white whales known as belugas had made the Saint-Laurent River their home, but they were endangered due to chemicals found it the water. They'd survived people hunting them near to extinction but they were still in jeopardy due to human activities and knowing Melodie was among those who fought for their survival made her feel closer to her.

Ana jumped when she heard glass shattering inside the inn.

"Oh my god, did you hear that?" Melodie called out as she pushed the bathroom door open and grabbed Ana's arm again, this time much tighter.

"Yes. It sounded like it came from the basement."

"Should we go check it out? Do you think water is coming in?" Melodie shrilled, squeezing her arm so hard Ana winced with pain.

"Water is probably coming in, yes, but we should definitely not go check it out. We need to stay on this side of the inn and out of the basement."

"Okay," she granted with exaggerated nods, not releasing her grip on Ana's arm. "What are we going to do, then?"

"Nothing," Ana replied as she used her hand to unclasp Melodie's fingers from her arm, convinced she'd bruise. "We're going to sit together and wait it out. There's nothing else we can do, really." She guided her toward the bed where they sat side by side, their backs against the headboard. Melodie entwined their fingers together and held tight, but the grip was more reassuring than painful now, and Ana welcomed it. There was a lit candle on each nightstand and the flashlight lay between them on the bed. There wasn't anything else they could do. The tide would eventually go down. The storm would pass. All they had to do was wait it out. She heard a banging noise against the north side of the building. Waves knocked against the porch and the wall of the inn. The sea had arrived and it wouldn't wait for an invitation to come in.

"It's definitely coming in, isn't it?" Melodie asked, panicked.

"Yes, it is."

Melodie sighed. There was no way she would sleep while the sea was taking over her property, and there was nothing she could do until the storm passed. She'd go crazy. Her cell phone chimed in and she reached out to grab it on the nightstand. A text message from her grandmother appeared on the screen.

Are you okay?

She wanted to tell her how terrified she was, how she'd heard a window break and water was most likely flooding the basement. Not to mention the damages it was making to the porch and the back of the inn. But all that would achieve was to make her grandmother feel as scared and powerless as she felt. So instead, she decided to be as reassuring as she could manage to be in her circumstances.

I'm fine. Ana is here with me. We'll call you when it's over.

Her grandmother replied with a thumb up emoji and she put the phone back on the nightstand. She sighed again.

"That was Yvonne, wasn't it?"

"Yes."

"She must be worried."

"Of course. But I told her we were together and we'd be fine."

"Good."

They both jumped and gasped when they heard a strong wave crash against the inn and another window break. "I hope I didn't lie to her."

"You didn't. We'll be fine," Ana said reassuringly before she covered her hand on the bed. Her palm was warm and soft. Her fingers were long and easily enveloped her entire hand. The sound of water swishing around in the basement confirmed their fear. There wasn't much to ruin down there, except for the laundry room. The washer and dryer were ancient, but they still worked. Until now.

"Well, the good news is that we won't hear another window break in the basement," she said as she shook her head, trying to chase away thoughts of the damages being done under her bedroom floor.

"We won't?"

"Nope. There are only two windows down there and they've both been smashed already."

"Oh, well, that's a glass half full way to look at it, I guess." Ana shrugged and they glanced at each other before they laughed. Melodie fixed her gaze on Ana's green eyes. They were darker in the candlelight, and she found a glimpse of peace in them.

"I'm grasping at straws here. Please help me. Tell me our place will still be standing in the morning."

"It will. The tide will go down soon. We're in the worst of it now. I promise."

Ana squeezed the hand she still covered and Melodie believed her. Ana was stating facts, and she'd never found science so comforting. "Is that why you're so calm? Because you understand exactly what's happening right now and how it's happening?"

"It helps, but I'm not all that calm inside. There are always variables we can't predict. I guess I'm grasping at straws too. Except my straws are the things science has taught me. Like the fact that the tide reached its highest point a few minutes ago and it has to start going down soon. That's the way tides work."

"I like your straws better than mine." They chuckled again and Melodie moved closer to Ana. She turned her hand under Ana's so she could entwine their fingers together again and she rested her head on her shoulder. "Tell me more."

"More about what?" she asked as she rubbed Melodie's hand with her thumb.

"More about science. Tell me again why you think we need to move away from the coastline. Call me crazy, but I suddenly feel more open to the idea now that the sea broke into my basement."

Ana laughed quietly, her shoulders moving up and down. Melodie closed her eyes and let her head bounce with the movement, finding solace in it.

Ana remained quiet for a few seconds after she'd stopped laughing. She didn't want another fight. Not now. She barely had enough energy for the fight that was already going on inside her. The battle to remain calm and strong. To be there for Melodie. She didn't want to take advantage of Melodie's vulnerability to convert her to her beliefs, but she did want to appease her, which talking seemed to do. So she decided to proceed with caution. "I really don't see what else we can do. The protective walls they talked about in your article, they're not here now. They can't help us tonight, and even if we started working on plans and financing tomorrow, I don't think anyone could build them before the next storm either."

She waited for a reaction. When none came, she took a deep breath and continued, keeping her voice low, her tone even. "But to me what's most important is that we're here now, in this mess, because we didn't respect the sea in the first place. We built our homes too close to it. We destroyed its beaches. I really have a problem with fixing what we've done by being even more disrespectful. By building huge walls or other structures that will mess with the sea in even worse ways. And for what? For our own little comfort? The problem with humans is that we think we belong everywhere and everything on this earth belongs to us. But it's not true. We need to learn from our errors. We need to learn to back off." She waited again until Melodie finally lifted her head from her shoulder and met her gaze. She didn't seem angry, and she didn't let go of her hand, which she saw as a good sign.

"So by moving away we wouldn't be running away. We'd be backing off. Giving back to the sea what belonged to her in the first place."

Ana smiled at Melodie's use of "her." The sea was female in French. *La mer*. She loved how everything had a gender in French, but she loved that the sea was female most of all. "Exactly."

Melodie let go of her hand only long enough to face her. She sat cross-legged and carefully placed the pink robe on her lap to ensure nothing above her knees would be exposed. Ana was grateful she didn't seem to worry about tightening the robe on her chest to cover the cleavage Ana glanced at as discreetly as she could while Melodie took her hand back and caressed her arm.

Ana wondered if she was this touchy-feely all the time and with everyone or if it was due to the situation. Or to her. She decided it was probably the way she was. Yvonne was the same way. They were an affectionate family, something she'd never known. She couldn't help thinking, however, that the circles Melodie was now tracing on her arm were much more intimate than Yvonne's casual hugs or pats on the back. "You see, I can understand things when I really want to," Melodie said with a coy grin that, mixed with the movement of her fingers on her arm, sent a jolt of pleasure down her stomach.

"I do see," she admitted as she took another glimpse of Melodie's deep cleavage. She noticed a large freckle on the inner side of one breast and swallowed.

"But what if we wake up tomorrow and everyone on the planet stops using gas. What then? Could we keep the sea from rising if we did that?"

The question startled Ana and she raised her gaze to meet Melodie's inquiring expression. Just in time, she thought. She didn't know what she would have done next, but she'd definitely been about to do something she could have regretted. She cleared her throat before she answered. "I wish that would happen. It needs to happen if we ever want the earth to start cooling down again. That said, even if we stopped using all fossil fuels tomorrow, it would take centuries before the planet cooled down again, decades before the climate simply stabilized. Don't get me wrong, stopping fossil fuel usage to stabilize temperatures in a few decades is still worth it. It's necessary, but it won't keep the sea from rising to levels we're not equipped to deal with. We're past that, unfortunately."

Melodie held her gaze and she tried to read her expression, tried to guess if she would blow up in fury any time soon. Instead, she sighed and smoothly declared, "Anyone ever told you you're a real party pooper?"

"All the time. I call it realistic." They chuckled and Ana took Melodie's hands in hers, holding them firmly before she added. "But I'm not a defeatist. I still think we can get it together and do the right thing. For Thomas. For his kids and his grandkids."

Melodie smiled. She wasn't sure what she'd think in the morning, but right now everything Ana said made perfect sense. She trusted her judgement, appreciated her honesty, and admired her faith in humanity. Melodie didn't have much faith in anything. Certainly not in humanity. But in this moment she felt like she could put her faith in Ana. She listened for the sound of water moving in the basement and heard nothing. Waves were no longer hitting the back wall of the inn. Winds were still powerful, but the sea had started to withdraw. "It sounds like you were right. The tide is going down."

"It is," Ana repeated as she let go of her hands. "The worst of it is over now. Do you want to go check out the damages?"

She made a move to get off the bed but Melodie stopped her by grabbing her arm. "No. It can wait until morning. We won't see much of anything in the middle of the night. Besides, I'd rather try to get some sleep."

"All right. I'll leave you to it then."

As Ana started getting up again, winds made the window crack and startled Melodie. She instinctively tightened her grasp on Ana's arm instead of letting her go. "Would you mind staying? I know I'm being a baby, but I don't think I'll be able to sleep alone tonight."

Ana settled back on the bed and smiled at her. "Sure. No problem. Lie down. I'll put you to sleep with my science stories."

Melodie snorted a laugh but obeyed. Ana blew out the candles before she lay on her back next to her. Without thinking about it or giving Ana a chance to protest, she wiggled closer to her and placed her head on her chest. "If you don't mind, I think this will work better."

"Oh, okay," Ana whispered before she wrapped her arm around her shoulders. Melodie could hear Ana's heart beat faster for a few seconds before it slowed again. She put her hand on Ana's stomach and closed her eyes. She let the rhythm of her pulse and breathing soothe her. They were strong and steady, and soon she drifted to sleep.

CHAPTER TWENTY

Ana woke up to the sound of a French tune. She recognized Edith Piaf's voice and wondered where it could be coming from until she realized the song was accompanied by a vibrating noise on the wooden nightstand. Melodie's cell phone. Melodie. She looked down and was shocked to find they were still in the same position. At first she'd been too aware of the weight of Melodie's head on her chest and the subtle movement of her hand on her stomach to go to sleep. She'd focused on remaining immobile and stoic. But then she'd finally relaxed and fallen asleep to the sound of Melodie's light snoring.

Sunlight was now coming through the curtains and Edith Piaf was insistent, repeating *Non, je ne regrette rien* over and over again. Ana looked at Melodie's small hand resting peacefully a few inches from the beluga on her chest, and she thought that she didn't regret anything about last night either, except perhaps what she was about to do.

She lightly jerked her shoulder and tapped Melodie's hand to wake her up. "Hey, your phone is ringing," she whispered.

"What?" she groaned in response.

"Your phone. It's probably your grandmother. She must be worried sick."

"Oh fuck," she said more clearly before she sat straight up in bed and reached for her phone. Ana took advantage of the distraction to get up and escape to the bathroom. Melodie might feel awkward about their sleepover now that the storm was long gone and Ana didn't want to face that possibility. She didn't want to know if the closeness they'd found through the storm would vanish now that things were back to normal. She didn't want to find out if Melodie would go back to hating her and everything she stood for this morning as easily as she'd relied on her through the night. She didn't want to know because it would hurt. She'd let her guard down to do the right thing, to keep her promise to Yvonne, and she might have to pay for it now.

She closed the bathroom door and flipped up the light switch only to realize the power was still out. She cracked open the door so she wouldn't be in complete darkness as she emptied her bladder. "No, I just woke up," she heard Melodie say in the other room. She expected to hear her speak French but she chose English, obviously for her sake, which could only be a good sign. She held her breath. "I'll check it out now and I'll call you back." A silence followed before she added, "Yeah, Ana is fine too. She's still with me. I'm so glad she was here." Ana let out a sigh of relief as soon as she heard the words. Apparently she was still in Melodie's good graces. "All right, I'll call you back in a bit."

Ana barely had time to pull her pants back on and flush the toilet before Melodie pushed the door open. "She can't get here this morning. Apparently some trees fell down and blocked the road. Is the power back on?"

"No," Ana managed to answer despite her total shock at Melodie's intrusion on her privacy. At least she was talking to her, she reminded herself. She seemed as comfortable in her presence as she'd been last night. She washed her hands with cold water. "I'll let you do what you need to do in here and then maybe we can go check out the extent of the damages?"

"Yes, that'd be great. I need to report back to Mammie in the next hour or so."

"Sounds like a plan. I'll wait in the other room." She smiled as she walked sideways to get past Melodie in the doorway, but she grabbed her hand to stop her.

Her touch was not the same as when she'd grabbed her arm the night before, panicked and terrified. This morning's touch was gentler, softer, and it sent shivers through her fingertips up her arm. She looked into her blue eyes, also softer than they'd been the night before. Melodie smiled and cocked her head in the most adorable way. "Thank you for staying with me last night. I don't know what I would have done without you." She punctuated her gratitude with a kiss on her cheek and Ana felt her entire face heat up under the innocent peck.

"No worries." *There's no other place I'd rather be*, she wanted to add. Instead, she continued into the bedroom and sat on the bed, patiently waiting.

They began their inspection in the basement, where they expected the worst damage would be. Ana led the way, holding the flashlight in the dark staircase and Melodie followed closely. Once they stood at the bottom of the stairs, Ana swept the space with the light, and Melodie sighed before she started crying quietly. Most of the water had already left the basement, channeled through the drain that was located in the middle of the concrete floor for that purpose, but the sea had definitely left its mark. A greyish film-like substance covered the floors and part of the walls. The smell of kelp, which Melodie usually identified as the scent of home, was so strong it became nauseating. Drawn to the light and fresh air coming through the two small openings left by the broken windows, Melodie walked toward the north side of the basement, but Ana blocked her way by extending her arm in front of her. "There's glass everywhere. You could get hurt."

"Right," she agreed in a broken whisper.

"Let's go back upstairs and see what it looks like outside," Ana proposed as she offered her hand. Melodie held on to it as she climbed the narrow staircase behind Ana. She couldn't get out of that space fast enough. They'd seen all there was to see already, except for the washer and dryer, which they wouldn't be able to test until the power came back anyway. She took a deep breath as soon as they got to the first floor. "Are you okay?" Ana asked as she let go of her hand and turned off the flashlight.

"Yeah, but I couldn't breathe down there."

"The smell is pretty bad, but the damages don't look too bad. We'll have to replace the windows and clean up everything. Perhaps replace the laundry equipment. Your grandmother has insurance, right?"

"Yes. It costs a fortune, but we do have it."

"Good. Ready to go outside?"

Melodie nodded. They went back to Melodie's room to retrieve their raincoats and boots and left the flashlight on the bed. Melodie glanced at the wrinkled sheets and wished she could go back to feeling safe and warm in Ana's arms instead of facing reality. She saw Ana look in the direction of the bed as well and noticed a blush cover her face when she realized she'd been caught. She wondered if Ana shared her wishes and felt her own cheeks heat up at the possibility.

As soon as they stepped outside, they walked into a thick spray mist and a taste of salt settled on her lips. They made their way to the back of the inn where the same greyish substance covered the entire porch and patio furniture. A few chairs had been thrown off and landed on the beach. The white paint covering the porch and the cedar siding of the inn had been damaged in several places, and the wood of two posts had been dinged, probably because of the chairs. Without exchanging a word, Melodie and Ana gathered the stray furniture back onto the porch. The residue the sea had left on them was thick and greasy. Once every chair was back where it belonged, they turned to each other. "What do you think?" she asked Ana.

Ana sighed, showing a sign of discouragement for the first time. "The entire porch will need to be sanded and painted. Same for the wall. Some posts and maybe parts of the floor and railing will need to be replaced. But I don't know much about carpentry. That's just my opinion."

"I think you're right. I'll ask my dad to take a look."

"Your father is a carpenter?"

"The best there is, when he's not too drunk to work."

Ana smiled with compassion and Melodie shrugged in reply before she turned to the sea. She was almost quiet today, as beautiful as ever, but she couldn't look at her the same way she had all her life. She didn't trust her, and she wondered if she could trust her again someday. She'd never been able to trust Aurelie again after her betrayal. Melodie was surprised at the thought. Logically, she knew both situations didn't compare. The sea hadn't lied to her or cheated on her. She'd simply behaved the way she was meant to behave. She didn't owe her anything. Ana was right: it was up to her to get out of her way. Yet this morning, as she looked at the mess her beloved sea had left behind her, she couldn't help but feel betrayed.

Ana watched closely as Melodie contemplated the Saint-Laurent. She appeared to be in some sort of trance, as if she was communicating with the waves. Oceans and sea levels had been part of her work, her obsession, for years, but she understood in that moment that all of her scientific studies would never compare to the bond that existed between Melodie and the sea. Her heart tightened as she realized for the first time what the retreat strategy she proposed truly meant to the woman standing next to her. It was as if she'd suggested Melodie had to leave a member of her family, or even part of herself behind. And Ana had done it so coldly, stating simple scientific evidence, without taking her feelings into consideration. Melodie had been right to think she might be heartless. She'd also been right when she'd implied that she didn't have any relationship of her own that could come close to Melodie's rapport to the sea. Ana had never known this kind of bond with anything or anyone. Not even her mother.

She watched tears on Melodie's cheeks and wrapped her arm around her shoulders to comfort her. Melodie immediately turned to her, wrapped her arms around her waist and sobbed quietly against her shoulder. Taken by surprise, Ana stayed immobile for a few seconds before instinct took over and she caressed her hair and back in a soothing motion. When the crying subsided, she dared to whisper, "We should go call your grandmother before she worries too much."

Melodie straightened up and looked at her with red-rimmed eyes. "You're right. Let's go back inside." But she didn't move. She kept staring into Ana's eyes, who held her gaze. "Thank you," Melodie finally said before she averted her eyes and walked toward the front door.

"You're welcome," Ana replied to no one.

CHAPTER TWENTY-ONE

It was mid-afternoon before the power came back and the road that led to the inn was accessible again. Melodie and Ana had spent the time walking on the beach and helping neighbors find and gather the belongings the wind and tide had taken from them. They couldn't find everything, of course, including Mrs. Vezina's cat, who'd never come home last night. They also made neat piles of broken trees, branches, broken furniture, and other debris. Some homes were damaged far worse than the inn. Others had remained practically untouched. The physical work helped Melodie keep her mind off the inn and the tasks ahead, starting with cancelling the few reservations they had for the upcoming weeks. The holidays would be spent mending their broken property.

Once they were thoroughly exhausted, they came back to the inn and shared ham and cheese sandwiches. They didn't talk. Their gaze met a few times and they exchanged understanding smiles, but they remained silent. Melodie wondered if Ana was as preoccupied as she was, or if she was simply giving her space.

Either way she was grateful for the quiet companionship. They were finishing their sandwiches when the electricity came back on. She hadn't turned on the light, but Melodie recognized the distinctive sounds of the fridge, the heat, all of that reassuring background humming one doesn't notice until it's gone. It was as if the inn was coming alive again, and she couldn't help but smile.

"That's a relief, huh?" Ana said as she covered her hand on the table. Their table. Melodie met her gaze and thoughts of the last meal they'd shared at this table rushed through her mind. That fight seemed so far away now. And so pointless. She smiled at her and nodded in agreement. "Would you mind if I went to my room for a hot shower?"

"No, of course not. I have phone calls to make. I'll be fine."

"You're sure?"

"Yes. There's no reason to be scared anymore, right? Go ahead. I'll clear the table."

"Okay. I'll be back in a few." She watched Ana walk to the stairs, still dressed in her sweatpants and Save the Belugas T-shirt. She'd put on a brave face, but she missed Ana's presence the minute she disappeared up the stairway. She realized she was being childish, but she couldn't help it. She cleared the table and turned on the lights of the lobby and computer. She was opening up their reservation software when her grandmother arrived with Miller. She almost ran around the reception desk to fall into her embrace. She thought she was done crying, but she sobbed as soon as she felt the strength of her grandmother's arms around her.

"It's all right, love. It's over now."

Ana got out of the shower feeling refreshed and ready to go. She wasn't sure what they'd do next, but she knew she wanted to do all she could to help Melodie and Yvonne recover from the storm. She couldn't explain why, but she felt responsible for what had happened, as if predicting it or even just talking about it had given her power to make it come true. She knew it was ridiculous, but she couldn't help it.

Melodie probably thought that now that she'd seen the storm, now that she'd lived through it, she'd simply leave and write about her experience and use it to prove that everyone needed to relocate away from the coast as soon as possible. She couldn't blame her for thinking that way. If the storm had hit at her arrival, that's probably exactly what she would have done. She'd be talking to governments and to various environmental organizations. She'd be using the sense of urgency the storm had created to make concrete plans, accelerating the process forward. She still planned on doing all that, but things were different now. Her priorities had changed. She cared about these women, about Thomas, about this place. She wanted to help them, to be useful to them first and foremost. She wanted them to know they could trust her. She wanted Melodie to keep relying on her.

She placed Melodie's sweatpants and T-shirt in a laundry bag. She'd wash them before returning them. She felt more comfortable in her own jeans, button-down shirt and sweater. She felt like herself again, yet she strangely missed the scent of Melodie's clothes on her and how close she'd felt to her while she was wearing them.

She heard Yvonne's and Melodie's voices as she went down the stairs. The first came from the dining room while the second came from the reception area. Miller greeted her at the bottom of the stairs with a wagging tail and she sat on the bottom step to pet him as she assessed the situation. Yvonne was on her cell phone, pacing back and forth in the dining room as she spoke in French. Melodie's conversation was in English, so she focused on her. "Again, I'm really sorry, Mr. Smith, and I hope you'll consider the White Sheep Inn for your next trip…right. Thank you and happy holidays."

She hung up and turned to Ana. "Feeling better?"

"Much, thank you. It sounds like that call went well."

"It did, but unfortunately they're not all as understanding as Mr. Smith. Some are downright nasty about it. No fucking compassion at all."

She raised her voice and Ana saw her eyes fill with tears. She rushed around the reception desk and put her hands on Melodie's shoulders. "Hey, why don't you take a break, huh? I'll call the next one."

"No, it's fine. It's not your job—"

"I insist."

Melodie met her gaze and took a deep breath before she smiled. "Thank you."

"No need to thank me. We're in this together." She picked up the phone but waited before dialing, distracted by Yvonne, whose tone had also changed. She sounded angry. "What's that about? She doesn't sound happy."

"She's with the insurance company. And you're right; it sounds like the conversation took a turn for the worse."

Melodie didn't explain further and she looked worried as she listened to her grandmother. Soon she joined her in the dining room and they both became more and more upset as the conversation went on. Ana called the next name tagged as English speaking on the list of reservations, a nice lady who wished them the best and promised to stay at the inn on her next visit. When she hung up, Yvonne was finishing up with the insurance company and both women looked completely defeated.

"What's going on?"

"Apparently those fuckers haven't covered flooding caused by natural disasters in this area for over two years. They say they sent a letter but Mammie doesn't remember seeing it and I sure haven't seen it."

"Did you pay for it?"

"We thought we did, but they say our premiums should have gone up and didn't because they stopped covering natural disasters. They say that alone should have raised a flag even if we didn't receive the letter, which they maintain isn't possible," Yvonne answered.

"Assholes," Melodie mumbled.

"Well, I'm sure the government will help in a situation like this. Right?" Ana suggested in an attempt to comfort them.

"It probably will, but that will take ages, like anything that comes from the government. If we wait for that money to fix this place, we won't be ready for the spring. Our busy season is short. We can't afford to be closed for any of it," Yvonne replied before she threw her cell phone to the floor.

Ana had never seen Yvonne so angry. For the first time, she recognized some of her granddaughter's temper. She didn't know what she could say to alleviate the tension, so she remained quiet. The silence soon became heavy as both women brooded over the problem. Ana stared at the next number on the list but didn't dare to dial it, waiting for someone to talk.

What broke the silence, however, was a meowing sound from outside. Ana immediately looked at Melodie, who met her gaze briefly before they rushed outside. They saw a black-and-white cat sitting less than ten feet from them and Ana instinctively grabbed Melodie's hand. "Do you think…"

"Yes, it's Mrs. Vezina's cat," Melodie answered as she squeezed her hand.

"Oh my god, I thought…"

"Me too."

They looked at each other and laughed nervously before they both crouched down and called the cat. "Here, kitty kitty," Ana called while Melodie simply clicked her tongue repeatedly. The cat ran straight to her and she picked him up. Ana caressed the fur on his back and felt him tremble. "Mrs. Vezina will be so relieved."

"Yes," Melodie said with determination in her eyes. She took a deep breath and massaged the thick fur around his neck. The cat stopped trembling and purred at the touch. "Everything will be okay," she added. Ana wasn't certain if she was talking to her, to the cat, or to herself, but she liked the assurance in her voice. She followed her inside and watched her take charge. "Mammie, call Mrs. Vezina and tell her we found her cat. I'll finish cancelling our reservations and then I'll call Kevin and Ana and I will go pick up dad. We'll get this place back in shape in no time. I promise."

"Come on, love. Do you really think we can count on Kevin and your dad to help us?"

"I won't give them a choice, Mammie. They owe us that much, don't you think?" She grinned mischievously and Ana couldn't help but smile in return, a strange mix of attraction and admiration brewing inside her.

CHAPTER TWENTY-TWO

Ana didn't know why she was needed to go pick up Melodie's dad until Melodie parked her Honda Civic in front of an old decrepit bar and explained. "I may need your help to drag him out of there. Depends how long he's been drinking already."

"What if he's home?"

"Oh he's here." She sighed and got out of the car so Ana followed. They entered the bar and were welcomed by a vile odor of stale beer and humidity. The ceiling was low; the room was dark. Ana tried to hold her breath as she followed Melodie to a round table where four middle-aged men played cards and laughed too loud. She recognized Melodie's father even before they got to the table. Those light blue eyes had to be related. *"Salut, Papa."*

"Ma belle fille," he exclaimed before he pulled her down into a hug, obviously happy to see his daughter.

"This is Ana, my friend." Melodie continued in English for her sake, which she was grateful for.

"Nice to meet you, Ana. Any friend of my daughter's is a friend of mine," he said with a thick accent as he stood up and shook her hand, holding on to the table with his other hand to steady himself.

"Nice to meet you too, Mr. Beaulieu."

"Please, call me Jerome." One of the other three men said something in French and they all burst out laughing again. "Don't listen to them. They're assholes," he added for Ana, slurring his words.

"I can't understand a word they say, so don't worry about them." They laughed again and Jerome fell back into his chair.

"Ana and I are here to take you back with us, Dad. We need you at the inn."

"You what?"

"I need you," she repeated, looking straight into his eyes. Ana knew enough about Melodie now to guess her father hadn't heard those words often in recent years, if he'd heard them at all. In fact, she would have been willing to bet that Jerome had needed his daughter much more than she'd needed him. The way they stared at each other confirmed her suspicion. Jerome finally nodded and stood up again, holding on to the table as he bid farewell to his drinking buddies in French. As soon as he walked away from the table, he staggered and grabbed a hold of Melodie to keep from falling. Ana rushed to his other side and put his arm around her shoulders. They carefully and slowly made their way to the car where Jerome quickly settled into the back seat and let Melodie secure his seatbelt.

Ana stood by the car and observed, shocked and saddened by the man's appearance in the light of day. His grey hair and beard were long and shaggy. His plaid shirt and faded jeans were crumpled and dirty. The smell of the bar clung to him. She focused on his eyes, the only part of him she found familiar and comforting. The sound of the car door closing startled her and she realized she'd been caught staring. "He's a different man when he sobers up, you'll see," Melodie declared before she walked around the car to the driver's side.

Ana took her place in the passenger's seat and offered
Melodie a compassionate smile before she drove away. They'd
barely made it two blocks when Jerome started snoring in the
back seat. "He hasn't always been this bad, if that's what you're
wondering." Melodie's words interrupted her thoughts. That
was exactly what she'd been wondering, imagining her own
childhood, as loveless as it had been, might have been a picnic
compared to Melodie's. "He's always been a heavy weekend
drinker, but he always found a way to keep a job while I was
growing up. We always had a roof over our heads and food on
the table. He was a great dad. The drinking wasn't out of control
before I left home."

"Do you think he might be lonely?" Ana asked, not realizing
her question might sound accusatory before it came out of her
mouth.

"I know he is," she answered with a deep sigh. "What was I
supposed to do? Stay with my dad and take care of him for the
rest of my life?" she added more defensively, raising her voice.

"Of course not," Ana hurried to say as she placed a hand
on Melodie's knee to soothe her. "Your father's an adult. His
happiness is not your responsibility any more than my mother's
happiness was mine." Melodie covered the hand she'd put on her
knee but Ana jerked it away and focused on the sea view out of
the passenger's side window. She couldn't believe or understand
why she'd brought up her mother into this conversation.
Constance's voice came back to her, replaying the words she'd
spent the last days of her life repeating over and over again.
Words that had validated Ana's impressions of her childhood.
Words she'd thought she'd buried for good when she'd buried
her mother. "I might have won a Tony award if I didn't have to
drag you around with me everywhere. The least you can do now
is take care of your dying mother. You owe it to me."

Ana remained quiet for the rest of the drive. Melodie gave
her the space she needed. There were hundreds of questions she
wanted to ask about Ana's mother, but now was not the time,
not with her drunk father in the back seat of her car. She wasn't

ashamed of her father. She knew he and Ana would get along once he sobered up and she would see what a great man he could be. Yet she couldn't help but feel embarrassment from the situation. She was still surprised she'd asked Ana to come with her. She knew she'd find her father in that bar, and she knew he'd be drunk. She could have asked Kevin to come with her. He was used to seeing her father that way and wouldn't have thought anything of it. But she'd asked Ana.

Kevin's pickup truck was parked in the driveway when they arrived at the inn and she rushed inside, followed by Ana. They found Kevin and her grandmother sitting at a table in the dining room, drinking coffee. "Kevin Cloutier, I told you that truck isn't safe for Thomas." She looked around for her son but couldn't see him anywhere.

"Relax, Mel. Thomas stayed home with my family. I wasn't sure what I'd walk into when I came here. I'll bring him back in my parent's SUV tomorrow."

"Oh, good," she said to express her relief, hoping she'd managed to cover her disappointment about his absence.

"Where's your dad?" her grandmother asked, worried.

"Sleeping in the car."

"Figures," she added as she shook her head. "I don't see what kind of help you think he can be."

"He will be fine, Mammie. We can put him in a room while we work on the repairs. He'll do the right thing. Have some faith in him, will you?"

"Stay here? With you, Ana, and the baby? No. I told you I'd take him in with me at the duplex. It's not your job to take care of him, love."

"It's not yours either. And it will be more convenient for him to stay here. Did you get a chance to look around, Kevin?" She closed the debate over where her father would live.

"Yes," Kevin said hesitantly.

"And can you help us fix things?"

"Yes. If your dad can give me a hand, we can get everything taken care of by the time I have to go back to Calgary in three weeks. Well, everything but the paint outside. You'll have to wait for summer to do that, but at least everything will be secured before I leave."

"Great. But you know we might not be able to pay you before we get money from the government. Will that be a problem?"

"Come on, Mel. We might not be together anymore, but we'll always be family. My time is yours. Just find money to pay for the building materials."

Her eyes filled with tears as she watched her grandmother hug Kevin to express her gratitude.

"I know nothing about construction, but I'll be glad to help any way I can," Ana added. Melodie turned to her and wiped the tears out of her eyes, unable to speak.

"I'm sure we'll find stuff for you to do," Kevin said as he approached Ana and introduced himself.

Melodie watched them shake hands and exchange pleasantries. She saw them laugh with her grandmother and surprised herself thinking everything might very well be okay after all.

"Want me to help you get your dad inside before I go?" Kevin asked, interrupting her thoughts.

"I can help," Ana offered, standing by her side.

Melodie met her gaze and had no doubt that she really did want to help. Although getting her father inside would be much easier with the help of Kevin's physical strength, she'd decided to share this difficult and sensitive part of her life with Ana today, and she didn't want to back out of that decision now. "You go back to Thomas and your family. Ana will help me with Dad."

CHAPTER TWENTY-THREE

On Monday, Kevin came back early with Thomas so they could get to work. The first thing on their list of priorities was to replace the two broken windows in the basement. Kevin had taped some tarp to cover the openings when he'd come to evaluate the situation, but that didn't suffice to keep the cold out and the heat in. They were losing precious energy, and to make things worse, temperatures had dropped dramatically since the night of the storm. So Yvonne went out with Kevin to purchase two new windows from someone who would give them a good deal while Ana helped Jerome remove what was left of the broken glass and the wooden frames. Melodie was upstairs with Thomas, cooking lunch for everyone.

Melodie was right. Jerome was a completely different man when he was sober. He was calm, attentive, and meticulous. He showed Ana what to do, taking the time to explain every move he made on one window so she could repeat them on the second one. If she did something wrong, he showed her again. He never lost his patience and Ana felt at ease with him. His hair was tied back in a ponytail and he wore a clean plaid shirt and jeans. His leather tool belt hung low on his hips. He seemed to take pride in wearing it.

Ana and Melodie had gone back to town the night before to gather his belongings from the room he'd been renting. They hadn't even filled a suitcase with his clothes and he didn't own anything else besides his tool box. When Ana had examined the red steel tool chest she'd finally been able to imagine the man Melodie swore was behind the drunk they'd picked up in that disgusting dive. Every tool was in a pristine state and in its place. Every screw and bolt was methodically organized.

"Now take out that last stop with the small crowbar like I showed you."

"Like this?" she asked as she delicately separated the last inside stop from the window with the crowbar.

"Exactly." He jerked the window out and pushed it on the ground outside. "All right then. We're ready to build the new window frames as soon as Kevin gets back. You know, if you're going to keep helping us like this, we'll have to get you better gloves."

She looked down at the gloves he'd given her. They were brand new, but much too large for her even though she'd always thought she had large hands for a woman. "You think?" she asked as she bent the empty last inch of one glove finger over her actual finger. He laughed and Ana recognized the loud, explosive laughter she'd heard a few times in Melodie. It was contagious, and she couldn't help but laugh in return.

"So how long have you known my daughter? She doesn't make new friends easily and I'd never heard of you before."

"Just a little over a week. I came to the inn for work, actually. Yvonne and Melodie have treated me well and we became friends." She didn't see the point in explaining the ups and downs of her relationship with Melodie.

"So you're a guest here?"

"That's right."

"So you don't have to be here right now, do you? You don't have to do this with us," he continued as he pointed to the tool box on the concrete floor. "What is it? You were dying to learn how to replace a window?" He laughed again, but this time nervously, as if he wasn't sure he had any right to question her intentions, which she found both sad and endearing.

"I know I haven't been here long, but I've quickly grown very fond of your mother, your daughter, and your grandson. Hell, I even have a thing for Miller," she admitted with a chuckle. He smiled and she continued more solemnly. "I want to help them in any way I can. That's all."

He nodded, apparently satisfied with her answer. "That's good. I want that too. I haven't been there much for them lately." He looked down and scratched his beard, embarrassed. "I guess I haven't made a good first impression on you, huh?"

"What are you talking about? You taught me how to replace a window. That's as good as it gets in terms of first impressions."

He laughed again, louder than before, and affectionately patted her back. She'd said the words to reassure him, but the truth was she'd practically forgotten the Jerome she'd met at the bar. She much preferred the man who stood by her now, and she wouldn't forget his kindness and generosity.

"I'm glad you're back," Melodie said to Kevin when he returned with one of the windows. "I don't know what's going on down there, but I hear more laughing than working, that's for sure," she said teasingly and loud enough for Ana and her father to hear from the basement. She couldn't hear what they were talking about, but her father's laughter was loud enough to travel through the floor. She smiled every time she heard it. It had been a while. Too long. "Where's Mammie?"

"She didn't feel good so I dropped her off at her house. She said she'd come back after she takes a nap."

"Okay," Melodie simply said, trying not to worry.

"She'll be fine," Ana said behind her. Her voice startled her because she hadn't heard her come up from the basement, but her hand on her back immediately soothed her. "She's probably a little tired, that's all."

"You're right."

"I hope you came back with more than that one window," her father joked to Kevin as he joined them.

"I did, and I could use some help getting it all out of the SUV."

"I'm right behind you."

Both men went outside and Melodie turned to Ana. "Sounds like the two of you are getting along."

"We are. Your father's a good man."

"Told you so," she replied as she took in Ana's appearance. The sleeves of her light blue shirt were rolled up to her elbows and the top buttons were undone, showing a white cotton tank top. Her shirt and jeans were dusty, and she even had a little sawdust on her face. Her hair was messier than ever, and for the first time Melodie didn't even try to resist running her hand through it. It felt softer than she'd imagined but was just as thick. She gently pushed the unruly hair away out of her face and smiled at the blush that instantly covered Ana's cheeks. She lightly rubbed the dust off her forehead. "Look at you, you're a mess." She meant to be playful but the words came out as a trembling, raspy whisper, surprising her as much as Ana. She cleared her throat and stepped backward to put some distance between them. "Don't you have a meeting this afternoon? You should go clean up before lunch. It's almost ready."

Ana moved the sleeve of her ridiculously large working glove out of the way so she could look at her watch. "I still have two hours. I really want to help put the new windows in. Unless you need help with lunch?"

"I'm good. Go make sure those windows get installed properly. I'm not sure we can trust those two." She winked at her and Ana grinned before she ran outside to help Kevin and Jerome carry materials inside.

Melodie stopped to take a look at Thomas on her way back to the kitchen. He was miraculously still sleeping in his bassinet. She'd moved the bassinet and the rocking chair to the dining room, closer to the kitchen and farther from the front door to keep him away from the cold. She'd be spending more time in the kitchen than at the front desk in the next few weeks so it made sense.

She stirred the beef and barley soup that simmered on the stove. It was a good thing she and Ana wouldn't have much time alone as long as the repairs went on and her father stayed at the inn. She didn't know how long she'd be able to keep her distance otherwise. The more Ana got involved in their lives and the more she interacted with everyone Melodie loved and helped them as if it was the most natural thing in the world, the harder it became to remember she was not here to stay.

CHAPTER TWENTY-FOUR

Ana had volunteered to shop for a new washer and dryer with Yvonne. One week after the storm, they'd replaced the windows and cleaned the entire basement. They'd even repainted the concrete floor and walls. Everything looked like new but they desperately needed to do laundry, and the guy Jerome had asked to come and take a look at the old appliances as a favor had confirmed what they'd all suspected. Seawater had damaged them beyond repair. So while Kevin and Jerome replaced parts of the porch and Melodie stayed at the inn with Thomas, Ana took Yvonne to the appliance store. Yvonne immediately went to the least expensive washer models.

"You're running an inn, Yvonne. That thing's fine if you're doing laundry for two people, but don't you think you should get something a little more...robust? Why don't we go take a look at the industrial models over there?"

"We can go look at them if you want, but I can't afford them," she objected as she waved her hand dismissively.

"Humor me."

"All right, if you insist on torturing me."

They'd been looking at the larger capacity models for no more than thirty seconds when a young man came to explain all of their advantages. As if his age didn't already give away his lack of experience, he also seemed nervous, fidgeting with the hem of his cheap suit jacket and speaking so fast it was difficult to follow. Ana smiled as she watched Yvonne's eyes sparkle at his description of one particular washer's durability and convenience, her face lighting up at the mention of its steam feature, which could de-wrinkle clothes among other things.

"We'll take it," Ana declared. "And we'll take the matching dryer too, as long as you can deliver both of them this afternoon. Can that be arranged?"

The young man smiled and stuttered with such enthusiasm that Ana figured it had to be his first sale. "R-r-r-really? That can p-p-p-probably be arranged, Miss. I'll go check with my m-m-m-manager."

Yvonne swatted her shoulder as soon as the salesman walked away. "Ouch! What was that for?"

"Come on, Ana! Those machines cost twice as much as I budgeted and you know it."

"But you need them."

"No, I don't need them. I want them, but you know as well as I do that what you want and what you can afford are often two very different things. What I need is a washer and dryer and the ones I first looked at will do fine."

"No they won't. You'll have to do four times as many loads and make four times as many trips up and down the stairs to the basement. Please let these machines do the work for you."

"Are you deaf? I can't afford them."

"I'll pay for the difference."

"Absolutely not."

Ana sighed. She'd known the minute she'd volunteered to go to the appliance store that she'd contribute to the purchase. She still had plenty of money from the sale of her mother's condo and she wanted to do this for Yvonne and Melodie. She also knew, however, that convincing Yvonne would be a tough battle. "Yes, I want to do this for you. Please let me. You haven't let me pay for my room since the storm and this is my way of thanking you."

"We're not taking money for your room because we're officially closed for repairs and you're working your ass off to help us with those repairs." She objected again with vehemence.

"You still lodge me and feed me for free. Please, let me help you."

The salesman came back before Yvonne could argue further. He looked calmer now. "We don't usually do same-day delivery but I spoke with my manager and we'll make an exception if you take the washer and dryer now."

Yvonne opened her mouth to protest but Ana walked in front of her and shook the young man's hand. "Deal."

"Great. I'll go get the paperwork ready."

"Perfect."

Yvonne didn't even wait for the salesman to walk away before she swatted her shoulder this time. He furrowed his brows in puzzlement but then left them alone. Ana turned to her. "Do you always beat up people who try to do nice things for you?"

"Only the stubborn ones. Don't you think you're doing enough for us already?"

"I promise I won't buy any more expensive appliances for the inn. But please let me do this for you. I can afford it and I want to do it. Besides, if we can get out of here soon, we could take a little time to go for a walk with Miller. It's been over a week since our last walk and I miss them. Kevin and Jerome can manage alone for another hour or so."

"That would be lovely. And Miller would be thrilled."

"So it's settled, then?"

"I guess so," she replied hesitantly as she slowly shook her head, her squinted eyes expressing rebuke at the same time as her grin communicated gratitude.

"Good. Do you want to look for a new fridge while we're here?" That earned her another slap on the shoulder, but this time she'd anticipated it.

They stopped at the inn to get Miller, his ball and his water bottle, and they walked on the beach in their usual direction away from the church. Miller ran as fast as he could in the fresh snow that covered the beach. A twenty-foot stretch of water along the shoreline was frozen, making it difficult to imagine the storm surge they'd experienced merely a week earlier. She could only hope people wouldn't forget. The sea appeared harmless now that it slept under a layer of ice, but the reprieve was temporary.

"We didn't get to talk about your meetings this week. Are things progressing the way you hoped?" Yvonne had caught her staring at the sea and probably guessed her train of thoughts.

"Yes and no. I met with the mayor and members of the council. Everyone agrees we need a plan, but their first priority is to help people who lost their home last weekend, which is understandable. My fear is that by the time they deal with those more urgent needs, plans to relocate others who just happened to get lucky this time will be put on the back burner."

"Isn't that what always happens? People respond to a crisis and then wait for the next crisis."

"Unfortunately, yes. And that's how we get in trouble." She sighed and smiled at Yvonne. "But I won't give up."

Yvonne grabbed her arm. "And you shouldn't. People might not act on all of your recommendations right away, but you plant seeds in their minds. Melodie is proof of that."

"Melodie? What do you mean?"

Yvonne glanced at her and grinned. "I suppose she's too proud to tell you, but I think you're getting through to her. She's been asking me all kinds of questions about my vision for the relocation of the inn to that piece of land up the hill."

"Really?"

"Really," she confirmed as she bumped her hip playfully.

"That's good news, but to be honest I think her change of mind has more to do with the storm than with me."

"I don't agree. Sure, the storm scared the hell out of her. But I think if you hadn't been here, she'd be fighting for a protective wall right now. She would never consider moving away as a solution without your input. You planted the seeds in her mind. Keep doing that, Ana. It may not work as fast as you want it to, but it works."

"I'll keep at it, don't worry." She threw the ball for Miller, who took off like a rocket. "He's getting in shape."

"Yes, thanks to you."

Ana hesitated before she asked her next question. "And what about you? How are you feeling, Yvonne?"

"Tired, mostly. I don't know if it's the stress of the repairs or my Parkinson's acting up, but I have no energy. I feel nauseous and dizzy at times and I have to lie down until it passes. I feel so old, Ana. I would never tell Melodie or Jerome because they need me to be strong for them, but that's how I really feel. Old and weak."

Ana heard the frustration in Yvonne's voice and understood the implication of her confession. She was probably the only person she could share her vulnerability with. She put her arm around Yvonne's shoulders and lightly squeezed. "Why don't you make an appointment with your doctor? I'll go with you. Jerome and Melodie don't have to know."

Yvonne let her head fall onto her shoulder. "Thank you. You're so good to me. I don't know if I've told you before, but I'm so grateful you came to the White Sheep Inn and we've become friends. You're special, Ana. Do you realize that?"

Ana laughed nervously. "I don't know about that, but I'm glad we've become friends too."

Miller came back with the ball and Yvonne picked it up as she wiped tears from her eyes. "All right then. Enough of this sappy stuff. We better turn around and get back to the inn. Jerome and Kevin need your help and I want to make sure I'm there when they come to deliver our new fancy machines."

"You're probably right. I better go help them before the porch completely falls apart."

They laughed and Yvonne handed her the ball, which Ana threw in the direction of the inn. They both watched Miller take off as they walked slowly behind him, at Yvonne's pace. The cold wind hit them directly in the face and instantly dried Ana's own tears.

CHAPTER TWENTY-FIVE

"Thank you, I got it from here," Melodie said to Ana after she helped her get her father to his room and onto his bed. It was becoming their routine. Kevin and her grandmother would leave around four, and that's when her father would take a shower before he opened his first beer. By the time they were done with dinner around seven he was drunk and falling asleep in his chair so they helped him to bed.

Ana nodded and left the room. Melodie took his boots off and placed them next to the bed. She couldn't remember ever seeing his feet in anything other than working boots. Then she kissed his forehead and left him alone, closing the door behind her. It was a strange routine, but one that made her happy nonetheless. Her father didn't drink all day while he worked on the inn. He was still sober enough to play with Thomas for an hour or so before dinner, and then they talked until he got too drunk and sleepy to maintain a conversation. She felt like she had her dad back. He wasn't perfect and would never be, but she enjoyed the time she had with him. She was grateful Thomas was getting to know him too. They were making memories she didn't think they'd have and that was worth the trouble of putting her father to bed every night.

She went back to the dining room where she saw Ana sitting with Thomas in the rocking chair. He was sleeping peacefully in her arms and Ana was staring at him with a smile on her face. "That would make a beautiful picture," she said as she approached and pulled a dining chair to sit close to them.

"He's knocked out. He has so much fun playing with his grandfather."

"I know, but I should wake him up. I can't put him to bed before I feed him."

"Oh no, he looks so comfortable. Let him sleep for a little while. He'll get hungry soon enough and he'll wake up on his own."

"Don't you want to go to bed?"

"It's not even seven thirty yet. Come on, stay with me. Let me hold him a little longer."

"Sure, I just thought you were exhausted after a day working outside. You go to bed early every night."

"I go to my room early every night. That's different. When you all get ready for bed I go upstairs, but I don't go to sleep right away. I read or I work on my article until ten or eleven."

"Really?"

"Really." Melodie chuckled. "What's so funny?"

"I was sure you were going to sleep right away or I would have stayed up. I don't go to sleep this early either. I read, plan my menu for the week, surf the net, keep myself busy until I feel sleepy."

"So you don't mind keeping me company then?"

"No," Melodie said sincerely.

She didn't mind it at all. She was delighted to find herself alone with Ana again. It hadn't happened since the storm, although the connection they'd made that night was still there. She'd noticed it every time they exchanged understanding glances, in the way they did dishes together after dinner, or in the occasional encouraging pat on the back or soothing squeeze of a hand. What would happen if they spent more time alone now? Melodie was almost as scared as she was excited to find out. "Mammie told me what you did at the appliance store," she whispered, still moved by Ana's generosity.

"Please don't give me a hard time about it. I already had that fight with Yvonne and I won," Ana said playfully.

"I don't want to give you a hard time. I want to thank you. That was very kind of you," she explained as she placed a hand on Ana's knee. And there was the danger. She'd gotten physically close to Ana the night of the storm because she was scared. She hadn't thought twice about holding on to her that night or letting her hold her. It had seemed natural then. It shouldn't feel so natural now that they were safe. She had no reason to keep touching her every chance she got, yet she couldn't help it. And although Ana rarely initiated physical contact, she never rejected it. She seemed to welcome it and even encouraged it, like she did now when she covered her hand with her own.

"I'm glad I could help." Her green eyes showed sincerity and Melodie was drawn to them until she focused her attention on something else over Melodie's shoulder and the spell was broken. "I've been curious ever since I got here. Does anyone ever play that piano?"

Melodie scoffed. "No. It was my great-grandmother's. She was pretty good from what I heard but none of us play. Mammie gets it tuned every year and that's the only time we hear it."

"That's a shame. Do you mind if I try it?"

"You play?"

"I used to. I haven't played in years but this piano has been calling me ever since I saw it."

"Well what are you waiting for? Go."

She took Thomas from Ana's arms and put him in the bassinet as Ana sat on the piano bench and pushed the fallboard open to reveal the black and white keys. She started with a few scales and Melodie stood behind her, watching her long fingers travel easily along the keyboard.

"Here, sit with me. I'll try something you probably know."

Melodie sat on one end of the bench and Ana started playing. The music did sound familiar, but Melodie couldn't identify it. It was light and sad at the same time, and it moved her. She knew very little about classical music, but she enjoyed Ana's delicate touch on the keyboard and the fact that *her* fingers were bringing back her great-grandmother's piano to life after so many years of silence.

Ana stopped when she hit the wrong key. "That was beautiful. What is it? You're right, I've heard it before but I really don't know what it is."

"That happens a lot with classical music. We hear it in movies and we think it's beautiful, but we don't really know what we're listening to. This piece is Pachelbel's Canon in D."

"I see. I'll remember it now. I promise. Play it again."

She did and she got further into the piece until she clearly missed a note and grunted in frustration. "I need practice."

"Well, I certainly won't complain if you practice on this piano every day."

"You won't?"

Melodie shook her head, suddenly dreading the day Ana would leave and the piano would fall silent again. "For as long as you stay here, of course."

"Right."

Ana swallowed and Melodie thought that perhaps she dreaded her departure as much as Melodie did. Perhaps she'd rather stay right here on this piano bench, their thighs pressed together and their faces inches apart. Perhaps she was dying to kiss her too, she imagined as she leaned in and brushed their lips together.

Ana gasped in surprise and Melodie froze for a moment, wondering if she'd misunderstood, until Ana pushed her mouth more firmly against hers and let out a heavy sigh of relief mixed with desire. She plunged her hands in the thick auburn hair at the back of her head and pulled Ana closer to her as she opened her mouth to taste her lips, desperate to deepen the kiss. Ana grunted again, but this grunt expressed hunger rather than frustration, or maybe both as they couldn't seem to find satisfaction in this kiss. Their tongues greedily explored each other's mouth, their breathing ragged; their hands crushing their bodies together. They clearly wanted more, starved for each other. As much as they wanted it to, this kiss couldn't channel all of the energy that had built between them since the storm.

Thomas cried and Melodie tore herself from Ana's mouth. They stared at each other, breathing heavily, until he cried louder. "Fuck," she finally said as she caught her breath. Ana laughed and brought a hand to Melodie's reddened lips. "I better go feed him."

Ana nodded. "Get him. I'll go get the bottle ready." She kissed her softly before she stood and disappeared into the kitchen. Melodie went to the bassinet and took an angry Thomas in her arms, comforting him the best she could until Ana came back with a warm bottle. Ana played the piano as she fed him in the rocking chair, and since he wouldn't go right back to sleep, she regretfully accepted that whatever had happened between her and Ana would have to wait until the next time they were alone.

"I'll take him to our room and play with him quietly for a few minutes before I read him a story. It's our thing, you know," she explained apologetically.

"I get it, don't worry. Good night."

"Good night."

Ana kissed Thomas's forehead before she kissed Melodie's lips again. The kiss was sweet, tender, and utterly frustrating. Melodie heard the piano for another half hour while she played with Thomas, and then the inn fell silent. She put him in his crib and lay down in her own bed, replaying the evening in her mind. Maybe it was a good thing they'd been interrupted before they went further than that ravenous, crazy hot kiss they'd shared. Ana wasn't here to stay and kissing her or having sex with her was nothing but a sure way to end up with a broken heart. Then again, wasn't it already too late to avoid that heartbreak? Maybe she was better off going all in. At least she wouldn't wonder once Ana was gone. She'd know exactly why she hurt so damn much.

CHAPTER TWENTY-SIX

"Are you sure you'll be okay? You don't have all of your family with you to help this time," Melodie asked Kevin once more as he secured Thomas in his car seat. She watched to make sure he did it well, but she resisted the urge to double-check. He straightened up to face her but left the car door open.

"My mother will be there, Mel. Come on, don't give me a hard time. I'm leaving next week and I want to spend some one-on-one time with my son before I do. You get it, don't you?"

"I do. Sorry. I can't help it. I know he'll be fine. You'll take good care of him."

"There. Did that hurt?"

He grinned as she brought her index and thumb an inch apart. "Only that much." He laughed and shook his head. "No, really, you're getting to be a pretty good dad. And you did an amazing job on the inn."

"It was fun working with your dad and Ana. We made a good team. If you paint the porch while I'm around this summer I'll be happy to help again."

"Thanks, Kev." She kissed him on the cheek before she kissed Thomas on the forehead and closed the car door. "Now go, before I change my mind and keep him with me."

"Right. I'm out of here. I'll see you on Sunday."

She stayed outside until the SUV backed out onto the street and left with her son. When she went back inside she saw Ana and her grandmother chatting in front of the piano. Yvonne had been so excited to find out Ana could play the piano that she'd begged her to use her talent every chance she got.

In the two weeks since they'd shared their first kiss, Ana and Melodie had had very little time alone. Her father and Kevin had worked hard to finish the repairs outside the inn before Kevin had to go back to Calgary. They'd worked through the holidays and Yvonne had stayed late to have dinner with them and celebrate as much as they could. No presents had been allowed for Christmas, money being tight for everyone, except perhaps for Ana. She'd been wise not to buy presents anyway. Yvonne still felt uncomfortable accepting the washer and dryer Ana had helped to purchase. Another present would have been too much for her to bear.

Her father made his appearance in the lobby. He wore his old brown leather jacket lined with black fleece, the trapper hat he'd had since Melodie was a teenager, and his working boots. "I'm ready."

"All right, let's go," Ana said as she stood from the piano bench and hurried to get dressed in her winter gear. Melodie's dad had planned a night out with his old drinking buddies. She didn't like it but she knew she couldn't keep him locked inside for the rest of his life. He hadn't left the inn in three weeks. He deserved a night out, as decadent and unhealthy as it might be. He'd promised to call when he was ready to come back home, but Melodie didn't expect to hear back from him until the next day. If she heard from him at all. "I'll be right back," Ana added for Melodie before she closed the door behind them. Ana had generously volunteered to drive him to town, and as Melodie watched them leave in a hurry, she was grateful her grandmother had stayed after dinner. She wasn't ready to be completely alone, not even for the half hour it would take Ana to drive her father to the bar and come back.

"Can you believe this old piano is useful again?" she heard her grandmother ask behind her, making her realize she was still staring at the door.

"She plays beautifully, doesn't she?"

"Oh yes. Will you come and sit with me while I finish my tea?"

Melodie followed her grandmother to the table closest to the piano, one she couldn't remember using before. She sat across from her grandmother and took the *Petit Beurre* shortbread cookie she offered. It was exactly what she needed: to bite into the comforting taste of her childhood as she watched her grandmother sip on her tea.

"I'm so glad you and Ana get along now. It looks like you've grown very close, actually." A playful sparkle lit her eyes and Melodie felt her cheeks heat up.

"We're good friends, yes." She'd thought they'd been discreet enough, but of course they hadn't fooled her. Yvonne noticed everything. It was infuriating.

"Friends, huh?"

"Yeah, friends." Yvonne took a bite of her own cookie and squinted at her. Melodie never understood why her grandmother's squinting eyes had the effect of truth serum, but they did. "Well, friends who might have shared a kiss one night."

"Ha! I knew it!" she exclaimed as she hit the table with her hand. "I see the way you two look at each other or touch each other when you think no one is looking. All I wanted was for the two of you to be friends, but this is even better." Yvonne's excitement was contagious and Melodie couldn't help but smile at her elation. Then she quickly remembered reality.

"How is it better, Mammie? Ana's going back home once her research is done. So where does that leave us?" She was surprised when her eyes filled with tears. She'd never expressed her fear out loud before, and saying the words made them almost too real.

Yvonne took her hands and looked at her straight in the eyes. "Oh, Melodie. And what if she stayed?"

"What? Did she tell you she wanted to stay?"

She lowered her eyes for a few seconds before she focused on her again to answer. "No, not exactly. But she's admitted what brought her here was more than her research. She felt some kind of mysterious pull to this place, to us. And I have to tell you, love, the more I see the two of you together, the more I think that pull was all about you. She came here for you, Mel. She doesn't know it yet, and I know you'll think I'm crazy, but I'm convinced of it."

She jerked her hands from under her grandmother's and crossed her arms on her chest. "You *are* crazy, Mammie. Ana's here to write about her relocation strategy. That's all." She shoved the last of her cookie into her mouth and chewed energetically.

"Yet what has she been doing for the past three weeks, huh? She went to what? Two or three meetings at most? She spent the rest of her time working on this place, taking care of all of us every way she could, buying appliances for us…kissing you."

Melodie swallowed her cookie and stared at her grandmother. "That doesn't mean anything."

"Oh please. Do you really think Ana's the type to kiss someone she knows she'll leave behind in a few weeks? Have you even talked to her about it?" Melodie shook her head in reply. "You know, dear, the way you took charge after the storm really impressed me. You didn't hesitate one second to ask Kevin and your father to help with the repairs, and I thought, good for her. She's not scared to ask for what she wants, and she gets things done. Don't stop now. If you want something more from Ana, if you want her to stay, ask her."

"But what if she says no," she said weakly as tears fell to her cheeks. Yvonne stood up and walked around the table to come and hold her. She dropped her head against her grandmother's chest and let her rock her gently.

"That's always the worst thing that can happen, isn't it? We spend so much time being afraid of that word. No. If she says no then you'll be hurt. But it's worth a try, don't you think? Won't it hurt just as much if you don't ask her?"

"Yeah, I guess it will."

Yvonne took her face between her hands and gently tilted it as she looked down, forcing their eyes to meet. "So you'll talk to her?"

"I will. I promise."

"Good girl." She kissed her forehead and then looked at her watch.

"It's getting late. You want to sleep here tonight?"

"No, I'll go back home. I didn't bring any of Miller's food with us and he must be starving. Besides, you girls need some time alone. You have all weekend to figure things out. Take advantage of it."

She walked her grandmother to the lobby and helped her put on her long winter jacket. They hugged tightly. When they broke their embrace, Yvonne caressed her cheek. "This makes me happy, Melodie. I really like Ana. And I love you, my dear girl."

"I love you too, Mammie."

CHAPTER TWENTY-SEVEN

Ana parked her car in its usual spot in the parking lot of the White Sheep Inn. She felt her heartbeat accelerate and she took a few deep breaths in an attempt to control it. This was ridiculous. She'd been alone with Melodie before. They'd managed an entire night and day alone during and after the storm, yet she'd been so calm then compared to now. Excitement and fear were battling to take charge of her heart and body. Excitement took the lead every time she remembered that kiss they'd shared on the piano bench, the kiss she'd thought about every night during the past two weeks. She'd kissed other women in her life, of course, but never like this. Every other kiss she'd experienced seemed calculated, expected, well orchestrated, as if it had been rehearsed from beginning to end before it happened. Kissing Melodie had been the complete opposite: an impulsive, spontaneous, clumsy but passionate expression of hunger and desire. She wanted more, but she was terrified of what it meant. And that's when fear took over.

What did this yearning and complete lack of restraint mean? Was this what falling in love was really supposed to feel like? Or had she completely lost her mind? She'd spent the last two weeks trying to tame her emotions, making a list of pros and cons about feeling the way she did. The long list of cons went from being uncertain of the reciprocity of her affection to the strong possibility of being hurt, not to mention having to move away from the stability she'd made for herself in Ithaca. The pros column was short but weighed heavily. It simply felt too damn good. So as she kept weighing the pros and cons, she began nonchalantly asking people she'd interviewed since her arrival in Sainte-Luce-Sur-Mer about possible positions at the University of Rimouski or the Maritime Institute of Quebec.

She took one more breath before she gave up on managing her emotions. The more she sat there in her car, the worse her turmoil became, so she might as well go inside and find out if Melodie was in a similar condition. She found the inn almost in complete darkness and felt nothing but disappointment at the thought that Melodie might have gone to bed. The letdown was not a happy feeling, but it had the merit of being clear and unequivocal. "Melodie?"

Melodie appeared in the dark hall and although Ana could barely see her, she recognized the pink robe she'd worn during the storm. "There you are. I was about to give that bubble bath another try. Come here and keep me company," she said before she went back to her room, leaving the door open for Ana. When Ana entered, she saw steam come out of the half-closed bathroom door. She got close enough to breathe it in and smiled at the familiar mandarin scent.

"Are you sure you wouldn't prefer enjoying your bath alone? I mean, without me on the other side of the door?"

"No, please stay. I won't be long. So how was dad? Excited to meet up with his buddies?"

"I guess so, but not as much as I expected him to be."

"What do you mean?"

"I'm not sure. He kept telling me the boys had insisted for him to come out, as if he was going out of obligation more than anything else."

"He was probably acting that way because he didn't want you to think he was looking forward to it. He cares about your opinion of him, you know."

"You think? Maybe. But at the same time I think he knows I wouldn't judge him." She felt dumb talking to a door and even dumber fighting the urge to peek inside.

"You can come in," Melodie said in a small, seductive yet hesitant voice, as if she'd heard her thoughts. "I'm covered in bubbles. It's safe," she added, her voice trembling now.

Ana went into the small, candlelit bathroom. She stood still at the sight of Melodie covered in bubbles and the pink robe on the floor. Her bare knee peeked through the white foam and she smiled invitingly. "What are you doing, Melodie? Are you trying to torture me?"

"Maybe a little," she admitted with a coy grin. "I'm getting desperate, here," she added playfully.

"Desperate, huh?" Ana prompted as she approached the bathtub.

"Yeah. I mean, what does a girl have to do to get a second kiss from you?"

"This may do the trick," she answered with a low chuckle as she knelt on the floor by the tub.

She pressed her lips to Melodie's and immediately felt Melodie's wet fingers slip through the hair at the back of her head. Melodie seemed fascinated with her hair and Ana enjoyed the way she pulled her against her mouth, as if she couldn't get close enough. Ana used her lips and her tongue to explore and taste Melodie. Ana's movements were slower and more methodic than they'd been during their first kiss yet there was nothing calculated about this kiss either. She simply wanted to take the time to savor what the frenzy of their first kiss had barely allowed her to taste. The urgent hunger of that kiss had been replaced with a languorous gluttony that was even more pleasurable. She took Melodie's lower lip between hers and lightly sucked on it as her tongue slowly travelled over its plumpness. Melodie moaned her appreciation and captured her tongue with her growing hunger. There was nothing polite about the way their mouths came together and for once in her life Ana welcomed the complete lack of inhibition. They grunted and moaned together until they were forced to break their kiss to catch their breath. They kept their mouths brushing against each other as they panted heavily.

"Do you think you could share my bathwater with me in it?" Melodie whispered as she began grasping at Ana's sweater.

Ana opened her eyes and noticed a slim rim of icy blue iris around enlarged pupils, dark with need. Her eyelids were heavy, her mouth open and reaching for her. "I'd much rather have you in it, actually," she answered in a raspy voice that betrayed the longing growing inside her own body. She jumped to her feet and stripped out of her clothes as fast as she could, without giving a second thought about exposing herself to Melodie.

Once she got in the water and felt her skin slide against Melodie's, she realized exactly what was going on and what was about to happen. She held her breath, panicked, but it was too late to turn back. She didn't want to turn back. She wanted Melodie against her and the way they threaded their legs together to get closer to one another, eager to resume their kiss. Water spilled out of the tub as they scooted their bottoms across the porcelain. They laughed at the mess they were making. They finally met in the middle and instantly stopped laughing, staring at each other as their breasts and stomachs pressed together. They didn't move, and Ana wondered if Melodie felt the electricity the contact sent though her body. She had to. They kept staring, their breathing becoming erratic. Ana's gaze went from Melodie's eyes to her mouth, half open and trembling, until she couldn't resist anymore and kissed her.

The kiss started strong and deep—they were way beyond tentative explorations. Ana felt Melodie's hands moving frantically from her hair to her shoulders, pulling her closer. She took a hold of Melodie's thighs, spread open and wrapped around her hips. She caressed her smooth skin under her thighs until she reached her buttocks, and in one quick movement she pulled her pelvis to hers. Melodie gasped at the contact of their centers. "Oh my god, yes. I want you so much," she whimpered as Ana kissed her neck.

Melodie broke their upper body contact to push her sex harder against hers, and as she leaned backward and rocked against her, Ana feasted on the sight of her breasts bouncing up and down with every movement. She caressed them with one hand as she provided support on Melodie's lower back with the other. She couldn't remember ever being this turned on, and although Melodie's sex crushing against hers didn't quite create the kind of friction she usually needed to climax, she didn't want it to stop.

"I need your hands," Melodie announced as she pulled herself back up to face her and put her arms around her shoulders, her mouth only an inch from hers, her eyes demanding as she added, "Inside." The plea aroused a need for her own core to be filled, and she inhaled sharply before she slipped a hand between them and through Melodie's folds. She easily identified the thicker, slippery wetness that coated the two fingers she pushed inside her. Melodie moaned against her mouth and kissed her. Ana barely moved, letting her dictate the rhythm with a subtle rocking of her hips, slow at first then faster before she slowed down again. Ana kissed her, caressed her back and her sides with her free hand. They fit perfectly. She placed her thumb against Melodie's clitoris, and she moaned again before she rocked faster. Her breathing became louder and heavier, and Ana knew there would be no slowing down this time. She slid a third finger inside her and used her thumb to rub her hard bundle of nerves faster.

Ana took pleasure in knowing she was about to give Melodie an orgasm but she was shocked when Melodie's hand slipped between them and easily found her own wetness. She knew she was ready but didn't expect to be so responsive to her touch, soft yet assertive—and so exactly what she needed. She quickly caught up to Melodie's momentum and they came together in loud and free grunts, moans, and whimpers. Melodie let her head fall onto Ana's shoulder, and they wrapped their arms around each other. They stayed in their afterglow embrace until Ana noticed goose bumps on her arms. "I'm getting cold. Are you?"

"Freezing." They laughed before Melodie added, "Let's get to bed."

They got out of the bathtub and didn't take the time to dry their bodies with a towel or pick up their clothes from the floor. Instead, they rushed to the warm sheets of the bed where they made love again. They explored each other with their eyes, their hands, and their mouths. They shared several orgasms before they finally rested side by side, facing each other. Melodie playfully twisted a lock of Ana's hair around her finger and she enjoyed the gentle touch as she used her own fingers to lazily trace circles on Melodie's hip. The desire in Melodie's eyes had been replaced with satisfaction at first, but now there was a hint of sadness in them too. "Are you okay?" she asked, scared of the answer.

"I'm more than okay," she said before she kissed her softly. "Just a little worried."

"About what?"

Melodie sighed and turned to lay on her back. "Forget it. I don't want to talk about it now. Tonight has been perfect so far and I want it to stay this way."

Ana rolled to her stomach and propped herself up on her elbows so she could look into her eyes. "Tell me what you're worried about and then we can go back to being perfect."

Melodie giggled nervously. "No, I'm going to sound needy and it's way too early for that."

"Too early? Is there a time to sound needy? Do we have to wait until midnight? Should I set up an alarm or something?"

She swatted her arm. "Stop it. Too early into our relationship I mean. If that's what this is." She grunted with frustration. "Damn shit! I said I don't want to talk about it."

"Well, we're talking about it now so we might as well get it over with," Ana replied playfully, acting as if she didn't know what Melodie was worried about. She was worried about the exact same thing, so of course she knew. "What is it you want to say that's going to make you sound needy?"

"All right. I'll tell you. I'm terrified what we started tonight won't go any further because you'll go back to Ithaca and forget about me." She cringed. "See how needy that sounds? I mean, we just had sex, right?"

"Is that all it was?" Melodie met her gaze and Ana hoped she could see what they'd done was well beyond sex to her.

"No. Not to me," she admitted before she bit her lower lip and swallowed nervously.

"Not to me either. Don't get me wrong. It was great, mind-blowing sex, but it was a lot more than that."

"So what does that mean?" Melodie asked as she turned to her side and held her head up with her hand.

"It means I want more. We both want more. Right?" Ana asked.

"Right. But how do we get more if you go back to the States?"

"That's not going to happen for a while. I still have a lot of people to interview."

Melodie clicked her tongue and sighed, annoyed. "That's still temporary. And that's what worries me. That you might stay long enough for me to fall head over heels for you and then you leave anyway."

"It's not what I want, Melodie. I've thrown in a few lines, I'm testing the waters, but I don't have any answers yet. I can't make any promises."

"Throwing in a few lines? What do you mean?"

"I've asked around about possible jobs."

"You have?" Her eyes lit up and she moved her free hand to Ana's side. She nodded in reply. "So you think you might like to live here? Like, for good?"

"Well I might not live in a hotel forever, but in Sainte-Luce-Sur-Mer, yes. Or Rimouski. Close to you." She barely had time to add this before Melodie shut her up with a kiss that communicated excitement, hope, and gratitude all at once. Her mouth became more insistent as her breathing grew uneven and Ana understood Melodie wanted her again, perhaps as much as she wanted her. They let their minds and bodies hope in a future together until they were satiated.

Ana drifted to sleep when she heard Melodie's phone ring. Jerome, she thought. She dreaded having to tear herself away from bed now, get dressed and drive to town to pick him up in the middle of the night. Only then did she notice light seeping through the curtains. It was morning. No wonder she was so tired. She started getting up as Melodie answered her phone but stopped in her track when she heard a panicked "*Quoi?*" She turned to her and read the same panic in her eyes, her face as white as the sheets. A few more words in French and she finally hung up.

"What's going on? Did something happen to your dad?"

"No. He walked to Mammie's and spent the night there. They got up early and she cooked breakfast but then she fell down, complaining about chest pains, so he called the ambulance. They're at the hospital now. They think it was a heart attack."

"Let's go. I'll drive." They scrambled to find clothes and hurried to get out of the inn. When they sat in the car, Ana put her hand on Melodie's thigh and whispered, "She'll be fine. She'll be fine." She hoped Melodie believed her more than she believed herself.

CHAPTER TWENTY-EIGHT

Melodie found her father in the small waiting room of the Coronary Care Unit of the hospital. He stood and opened his arms. She fell into his embrace and held on to him as she felt his body shake against her. He seemed as terrified as she was. "How is she?"

"They're doing all kinds of tests now. She might need surgery."

"Oh my god."

"Good thing you were there," Ana added. Jerome nodded and squeezed her hands gently before releasing them.

"Can we see her?" Melodie asked.

"Not now. They said they'd call us when we can see her again."

"What happened, Dad? What did the doctor say?"

"A heart attack. A big one. That's all I know, baby."

They hugged again and sat side by side, holding hands. Ana stood in front of them. She seemed nervous. She ran her hand through her hair a few times before she finally offered, "Can I get you anything? Coffee?"

Her father shook his head.

"No, thank you. Please sit with me," Melodie answered.

She did and Melodie immediately grabbed her hand. She thought she might find strength in holding both her father's and Ana's hands, and it helped, but she still felt scared. And lost. Her grandmother couldn't leave her now. They still had years to work together, to watch Thomas grow together. They had plans to move the inn up the hill. They still had time before her Parkinson's got worse. From the corner of her eye she saw Ana's leg bounce anxiously. She couldn't leave when Ana was trying to find a way to stay, when she could watch their friendship grow and see their relationship blossom. She so desperately wanted Mammie to see her happy and in love, to know she didn't need to worry about her anymore.

"I was bored," her father declared out of nowhere, his eyes on the wall facing them.

"What?" she prompted him to explain.

"I was bored with the boys at the bar. It smelled like booze and vomit, and they were acting dumb. I wanted to get back to the inn but I didn't want to bother you. So I walked to the duplex." She rubbed the top of his hand to encourage him. "She made coffee and we talked. We hadn't talked like that in years. We talked about the blue saltbox house on the beach. We talked about your grandfather a lot. We talked about you. I told her how sorry I was about not being a good son to her in the past few years." He started sobbing so quietly she wouldn't have realized it if his shoulders hadn't moved up and down.

"Oh, Dad," she simply said as she put her arms around his shoulders and pulled him to her. He cried against her chest as she patted his back lovingly. She could only imagine how happy her grandmother must have been after that conversation. Surely she wouldn't leave now that she could resume her relationship with her son.

Once he stopped crying, her father sat straight in his chair, got a tissue out of his jacket pocket and blew his nose. "She looked tired when she woke up this morning but she also looked happy. She insisted on making crepes the way she used to when

I was a kid. And that's when it happened." He fell silent then, staring at the wall.

Melodie turned to Ana, whose leg still bounced up and down uncontrollably. She placed a hand on her thigh to ease her anxiety and Ana turned to her. Her face was blank. Melodie tried to remember the way they'd lain in bed together. She knew it had been less than an hour ago, yet it seemed like a distant memory. Ana smiled weakly, but she wasn't with her. She was in her own thoughts, stuck with her own fears. She was probably thinking of her mother, who'd died less than a month ago. As bad as their relationship had been, it still had to hurt when she died.

A woman wearing a white lab coat appeared in the waiting room with a solemn expression and Melodie knew she'd lost her grandmother before she opened her mouth to speak. "Mr. Beaulieu?"

"Yes," her father said as he stood up. "What's going on? You can tell me, doctor. These young ladies are family."

"Your mother had another heart attack as we were prepping her for her electrocardiogram. It was a massive attack. Unfortunately we couldn't save her. I'm so sorry."

Ana froze as Melodie and Jerome sobbed, clinging to each other. She wanted to cry too, or at least find the strength to comfort them, but she felt powerless, incapable to control her own thoughts and emotions. She didn't understand the pain that settled in her chest. She'd known Yvonne for so little time. How could her death affect her to the point where she could no longer function? Jerome had lost his mother. Melodie had lost her grandmother. She'd simply lost a new friend she barely knew. Yet the heaviness in her heart was excruciating, far worse than anything she'd felt before. So much worse than the way she'd felt after her own mother had died. The realization sharpened her pain even more, making it difficult for her to breathe.

Thoughts of Yvonne and Constance inexplicably mixed together in her brain. Yvonne laughing as they walked together on the beach. Constance smiling at a stupid joke she'd told in an effort to distract her from the physical pain morphine could no longer alleviate in the hours before she passed. Yvonne grabbing her arm as they walked side by side. Constance squeezing her hand weakly before she took her last breath. She hated her mother for intruding on this moment. She wanted to be there to support Melodie, but once again Constance was taking over her life. Once again she was taking all the room in her head and in her heart. How could she still have that much control over her as she lay six feet under ground? She didn't understand what was happening to her, but thoughts of her mother rushed through her mind and smothered her until she suffocated and had to run from the hospital. She didn't say a word to Melodie or Jerome, still crying their loss as normal human beings did. She left and didn't look back. She ran. She needed to get away until she could make sense of it all. She took a cab to the White Sheep Inn, gathered her belongings and left nothing but a simple note on the reception desk. "I'm sorry."

CHAPTER TWENTY-NINE

Present

Melodie put Thomas back in his playpen when the Smiths stopped by the reception desk to chat with her as they had done every day of their weeklong trip. They were in their late seventies, perhaps even early eighties. They were both shorter than she and sported thick grey hair. His was straight and short, always neatly combed. Hers was tightly curled and never seemed to move or flatten, even after several hours of wearing a hat.

She admired the way they'd fallen into a routine so quickly, although they knew it was temporary. They ate breakfast at eight every morning. She ordered a croissant with homemade jam and he ordered eggs Benedict. They shared their plates and left half of both breakfasts untouched. Melodie had offered to cook them smaller portions for a lower price, but they always thought they were hungry enough to eat everything until they realized they were not. Miller didn't seem to mind their lack of appetite.

After breakfast they went upstairs to get ready for their visit of a tourist attraction they'd carefully selected in advance—

the Historical Maritime Site of Pointe-au-Père one day, the Regional Museum the next day, and so on. Mr. Smith had explained several times that they couldn't handle more than one a day. They ate lunch before they got back in the early afternoon and stopped by the reception desk to chat with Melodie before they went upstairs for a nap. Later they would go out for their daily walk and dinner. They were scheduled to leave tomorrow, and Melodie knew she'd miss them—although perhaps not as much as Miller. She'd convinced them to come back in the summer to visit the Métis Gardens. "I'm so happy we got to stay in this quaint little inn of yours, Melodie. We were worried after you called us to cancel last year," Mrs. Smith said as she had almost every day.

"I'm happy you decided to give us another chance too, but mostly I'm happy we didn't have problems with the tides this year." She'd given the same answer each day without much variation, but this time she couldn't help but glance at the article that was still sitting on the desk and a heavy sadness settled in her chest. If the Smiths left tomorrow as planned, she'd be left with only one guest. *Damn you, Ana.*

"Our visit of the churches in Rimouski was beautiful. It's such a shame we couldn't visit the cathedral. It looks beautiful."

"It is, but it's not safe for the moment. Don't worry, though, there are all kinds of plans to preserve it, so I'm sure you'll get to see it eventually." She knew that given their age and the time the city was taking to decide on the right way to preserve the historical church, they might not actually be alive to see any of those plans become reality, but she didn't want to break their hearts.

"Well, you have a good afternoon, darling," Mr. Smith said as he patted her hand. "We'll head upstairs now."

"All right, go and get some rest. I'll see you later."

She watched them climb the stairs slowly until they disappeared. She glanced at the article again, taunting her with its flared-up corner and catchy title. She shouldn't have kept the inn open for winter. If it had been closed and she'd been home at the duplex where she belonged, Ana would have been forced to go somewhere else or maybe even go back home and she wouldn't have seen her again. Ana wouldn't have opened that wound again. It had barely started to heal. How dare she come back after abandoning her during the worst possible time of her life?

She'd been so sad after her grandmother's death and so angry at Ana for leaving. She'd been convinced she'd lost her mind. Fortunately her father had been there to help her with Thomas. Kevin had also been a big help every time he came back from Calgary. They'd painted the outside of the inn in the summer and they'd had a great tourist season. Work kept her busy and eventually the pain became less dominant, leaving some room for laughter with her son, for light talks with her father or with Kevin. It had taken a long time but they'd started healing together.

Melodie had worried that closing the inn for winter would give her too much time to think. She wanted to keep herself busy. It had been difficult enough to remain strong as time brought them closer to the one-year anniversary of Ana's arrival, the storm, and her grandmother's death. Yet she'd managed to keep her composure until Ana's return. That night, she'd cried as hard as she had the day her grandmother died and Ana ran from the hospital like a coward. Then the next morning she'd decided she'd shed more than enough tears over Ana Bloom. She wouldn't let her get to her anymore. She'd ignore her until she saw there was no point in staying and left her alone for good. She wouldn't even fight with her or admit how much she'd hurt her. She couldn't let her see she had any power over her.

She took the article and hid it under the printer. There. Maybe if she didn't see it she wouldn't be so tempted to read it. Why the hell should she care what Ana had to say about her community? She'd left before she could help any of them put her damn ideas into motion. Some had already relocated. Others, like Melodie, felt powerless. She still believed it was the right thing to do, but she'd been too busy putting her life back together to make any concrete plans.

She knew damn well counting on the sea to freeze before the great tides every year was not the way to live. Ana had taught her that much. They'd been lucky this year, but they couldn't cross their fingers and hope to get lucky every year. She had to do something to preserve her family business and she couldn't take as long as the city was taking with plans to preserve the cathedral. Sea levels were rising and every future storm could potentially destroy everything they owned, including her grandmother's legacy. Maybe that's why she was so tempted to read that article. Maybe Ana's written words could show her the way without her actually having to talk to her, without admitting she needed her guidance. She couldn't risk her heart like that again. Ana was too dangerous.

She sighed with frustration and hit the reception desk with her closed fist. Reading that article was too dangerous too, though, wasn't it? Damn it. She'd find someone else to help relocate. Ana was not the only scientist around, after all. And Melodie was resourceful enough to find assistance elsewhere. She looked at Miller, who sat patiently at the bottom of the stairs, looking up every once in a while, waiting for her to come back down. "Stop it, Miller. We don't need her. Let's go for a walk."

She knew she had time to walk to the church and back before the Smiths came down from their nap, and she desperately needed fresh air. She dressed Thomas in his snowsuit and grabbed Miller's leash. She'd heard Ana make comments like, "you're getting fat, buddy. Let's go for a run." It was so infuriating. Maybe she didn't take him by the beach to run every day like Ana had since her return, but she'd taken him for walks two or three times a day ever since her grandmother had passed. She'd fed him, talked to him, petted him, even let him sleep in her bedroom. She'd taken care of him as well as she could for nearly a year despite her state of mind. She wouldn't let Ana make her feel inadequate. She'd run away. She'd abandoned Miller and the rest of them and she had no right to come back and act like a hero now.

Once outside she secured Thomas in his stroller and put her hand through the loop at the end of Miller's leash before she walked with the powerful energy provided by her frustration, pain, and fury. *Damn you, Ana.*

CHAPTER THIRTY

Ana heard the doorbell as she went down the stairs and saw Melodie, Thomas, and Miller come in, followed by Jerome. He was carrying his precious tool belt and father and daughter were in the middle of a conversation in French so she waited at the bottom of the stairs. His hair was still long, held in a ponytail. His beard was neatly trimmed, which was a change for the better, but the biggest change was in his eyes. They were clearer and brighter than she remembered. They took off their jackets and placed them on hooks behind the reception desk and didn't notice her. As soon as Melodie unhooked the lead from his collar, Miller ran to Ana and she petted him. Jerome freed Thomas from his snowsuit and put him on the floor as he chatted with his daughter and adjusted his tool belt around his waist. Thomas walked to Ana and petted Miller with an excited smile. She focused on the boy and the dog for a moment. When she looked back up, Jerome was staring at her, looking as pale and stunned as if he'd seen a ghost. Obviously Melodie had not told him about her return.

"Hi, Jerome," she simply said. Melodie turned at the sound of her voice but immediately made herself busy behind the reception desk.

"Hello, Ana," he said weakly before he quickly added, "I better go check on that toilet in room three." He stepped around her to reach the stairs and climbed them without turning back.

"Your dad looks good," she dared commenting, convinced Melodie wouldn't answer.

Instead, Melodie dropped the pen she'd been holding over a pile of paperwork, walked around the desk to pick up Thomas, and looked her straight in the eye. "He's doing great. We all are. So if that's what you came here to find out, you can go now." Ana watched her walk down the hall, standing straight and proud with Thomas in her arms. When she got to her room, she stopped in front of the door and turned back to call out in a light, energetic voice, "Come here, Miller." The dog obeyed and Ana was left alone in the lobby.

She wasn't here to make sure they were all doing well. She'd always known they'd manage without her. She was here because although she could, she didn't want to manage without them anymore. Sooner or later, Melodie would realize that. For the first time, however, she thought there was a possibility Melodie might choose not to take her back even once she understood all the reasons why she'd left and now returned. She shook her head. She wasn't ready to consider that possibility more seriously.

She climbed the stairs and noticed Jerome had left the door of room number three ajar. She hesitated for a few seconds before she pushed it open and slowly walked inside. "Do you need help?" she offered, her mind automatically going back to the basement windows they'd replaced together. They'd bonded then. He liked her then.

"Thanks, but I think I can handle it," he said as he turned off the water supply behind the toilet. The cover of the toilet tank had already been removed and rested on the floor. "I'll replace the flapper later but the problem now is that the tank level is too high."

"How do you fix that?" she asked.

"Easy. Simply need to adjust the fill valve." She watched as he reached into his tool belt and used a screwdriver to turn the screw on top of the valve. "There, that should do it." He turned the water supply back on and flushed the toilet to test it. It worked perfectly. He put back the cover of the tank carefully.

"Wow, that was an easy fix."

"Sure was," he said as he headed out. She thought she wouldn't get more out of him, but he stopped, sighed, and asked without turning to face her, "What are you doing here, Ana?"

The question surprised her but it was honest and she could only answer it as honestly, "I love your daughter, Jerome. I want to be here, with her."

He turned then and smiled weakly as his eyes filled with tears. "But why now? You broke her heart, you know?"

"Yes, I know," she admitted as she lowered her gaze.

"Why did you do it?"

That question was as honest as the first one but much more difficult to answer. She hesitated, ran her hand through her hair a few times, but finally decided telling Jerome was a close second to telling Melodie, who might never give her the opportunity to explain. She sat on the bed and found comfort in the fact that it squeaked exactly like hers. Jerome closed the door and stepped closer to the bed, facing her.

"You might not know this, but my mother died just before I came here last year." He nodded and held a finger up before he walked to the antique desk in front of the window looking out on the sea. He pulled the wooden chair that nested under the desk and dragged it in front of Ana. He sat backward on it, his arms crossed comfortably on the back of the chair, ready to listen. "My relationship with my mother was not the best. It was pretty shitty, actually. So when she died I didn't feel the need to mourn her. I didn't know how to mourn her, to be completely honest. How do you mourn someone when you're not even sure you're sad they're dead? I know it sounds awful, but that's how I felt after she died. So I left right after the service, came here, and got busy." He nodded again.

"But when Yvonne died, I was crushed. And then my mother's death got mixed up with Yvonne's in my mind and I couldn't take it. I was angry with my mother for coming back to haunt me that way, but mostly hurt. It was too much pain all at once and I ran. I'm not proud of it, but that's what happened. I had to get away from that hospital, from both of you, from all that grief. I had to figure out where all of it was coming from, and my instinct was to run away." A silence followed and she tried to read Jerome's expression but couldn't. "It doesn't make sense, does it?"

"Some of it does. You had to take the time to mourn your mother, and I guess you had to go back home to do that. What I don't understand is why you couldn't say that to my daughter before you left. You broke her heart," he repeated.

"I know. But I couldn't explain it to her then because I didn't know what was going on myself. All I knew was that I couldn't breathe here anymore. I had to go," she said before she started sobbing. She'd practiced her explanation so many times in her mind, but now that she was voicing it, she couldn't understand why she'd ever imagined Melodie would forgive her. She'd been selfish. She'd hurt her and there was no turning back. She felt Jerome's large hands take hers and squeeze them the way he'd done that day in the hospital.

"Were you able to mourn your mother while you were gone?" She nodded as she sniffled. "Good. I'm glad you did." She watched him reach for the box of tissues on the nightstand and hand it to her.

She blew her nose and he walked toward the door. "Can you forgive me? For leaving and breaking her heart?"

He turned to her again, sighed and smiled. "If Melodie can find it in her heart to forgive you, I guess I will too. But you have to understand I'll be on her side no matter what."

"Do you think she can? Forgive me, I mean."

He shrugged and left, closing the door behind him. She stayed in a room that wasn't hers to cry a little more before she could finally regain her composure and go back to her own room. Tomorrow she'd start looking for an apartment. She no longer believed she could be forgiven. She certainly no longer believed she deserved it. She'd get out of Melodie's hair for good. She owed her that much.

Melodie sat on the bed, playing distractedly with Thomas's stuffed rabbit while he slept by her side and Miller snoozed by her feet. She envied them. She'd thought the fresh air from their walk would bring her enough peace to close her eyes for a power nap, but she couldn't stop thinking about Ana and the article that hid under the printer. Hiding stuff didn't really work if you were the one hiding it, did it? She'd be tempted to read that damn thing until she put it through the shredder, and she couldn't bring herself to do that. She clicked her tongue in irritation. Then she heard a knock on the door and smiled. Her father knocked exactly the same way her grandmother had. Two quick strikes followed by a pause and one last, softer knock. "Come in, Dad."

He pushed the door open and whispered so Thomas wouldn't wake up, "The toilet is fixed." Miller was already up and wagging his tail. He stepped inside to pet him.

"Great. Thank you."

"I didn't know you still kept this room," he said as he looked around the space.

"I don't, really. I don't keep anything here anymore. I even rented it a few times this summer when we were full. But we still come here to rest once in a while."

"Or to get away from Ana." She met his gaze, annoyed that he knew her so well. "Why didn't you tell me she was back?"

She squared her jaw and averted his gaze. She hadn't told her father about Ana's return because it would have made it real and she refused to acknowledge it.

"It didn't come up, I guess."

"Come on, Mel. We share a house. We have dinner together every night. I'm sure you could have found a moment to tell me. Why didn't you?"

"Because I don't want her to be here. I don't want to talk to her or about her. I don't want to acknowledge her presence in any way. I just want her to be gone." She wiped away the tears that fell to her cheeks and grunted, angry to find out she could still cry over that woman. "Don't you think I've cried enough already? I don't want to talk about her, Dad. I want her to leave us alone for good."

"Then maybe you should hear her out."

"What?" she hissed furiously, insulted by her father's suggestion. He sat on the bed on the other side of Thomas, who turned his head in his grandfather's direction but kept sleeping.

"Hear her out. Let her explain what she came here to explain. I'm sure that if you still want her to go after that she'll respect your decision. She won't impose on you, baby. She simply wants to tell you why she left and apologize."

"Is that what she told you?"

"No."

She squinted at him the same way her grandmother used to squint at her, which she did more and more often. With her father, with Thomas, even with Kevin. "Did she explain it to you?"

"She might have. A little," he admitted.

"Then tell me. Let's get this over with. I'll tell her you shared her explanation with me and that it doesn't change anything and she'll leave at last."

"It's not my story to tell. Talk to her." He flattened his large hand onto Thomas's back, kissed his forehead, and stood up. "I'll see you at home tonight."

"You're really not going to tell me what she told you?"

"Nope," he answered before he left the room. She grunted and threw Thomas's stuffed rabbit at the closed door.

CHAPTER THIRTY-ONE

Kevin came to pick up Thomas before dinner that Friday. Father and son spent all their weekends together when Kevin was in town. Melodie was used to it now and trusted him entirely. She even wished he could find work closer to town so Thomas could spend more time with him. "Don't forget, he's super quick now, and he gets into everything," she warned as they stood in the lobby of the inn, Thomas dressed in his snowsuit and standing proudly by his dad.

"I won't let him out of my sight, don't worry." He still had that boyish grin that made him irresistible, but he seemed more mature at the same time. Or maybe she simply saw him that way. "We'll have so much fun snowmobile racing, right Thomas?"

She squinted at him and almost opened her mouth to protest but remembered how much he loved making fun of her overprotective nature and didn't bite. "Stop it."

"No, really. I bought a little helmet for him. He'll be my co-pilot."

She swatted his arm and he laughed. "You're such an asshole."

"Hey now, language," he protested as he picked up Thomas and she handed him a duffle bag full of clothes and toys. "We'll be back on Sunday as always. Let me know if you want me to drop him off here or at the duplex."

"All right, thanks. Be careful."

"Always." She opened the door for Kevin and closed it behind him right away. It was frigid cold outside. She no longer felt the need to verify Thomas's car seat every time they left, but she always watched them go from the small window in the door. She didn't think Kevin knew she was watching, or at least she hoped he didn't. He made enough fun of her already.

The Smiths came down the stairs, right on time, ready for their walk and dinner outing. "Be careful out there. It's freezing."

"We dressed warmer than usual. Thank you, darling," Mrs. Smith said as she walked by her. She opened the door for them and closed it with a heavy sigh. She wished she could go home, but she didn't want to break the Smiths' routine. She'd been there to welcome them back to the White Sheep Inn every night, all week long. She'd asked them if they needed anything before they turned in and they never did, but it wouldn't feel right to miss their last night. She wanted to be there for them.

Hopefully Ana would stay up in her room. She went back to the paperwork she'd put aside earlier, unable to focus. She still felt that pull toward the article hiding under the printer, and she couldn't get her father's words out of her mind. Hear her out. What if he was right? What if Ana only needed to speak her mind and apologize before she could leave them alone? What if refusing to hear what she had to say was akin to refusing to put her goddamned article through the shredder? What was she hanging on to so desperately?

"Fuck it. We're going to rip that Band-Aid off right now," she muttered to herself before she climbed the stairs two steps at a time and knocked on the door of room number one.

Ana was startled when she heard the loud, repetitive banging on her door. She'd been staring at the frozen sea out the window, quietly crying and beating herself up for thinking she could come back here and hope to be forgiven. She went to open the door and was shocked when Melodie walked past her, looking as determined as she'd ever looked. "All right, Ana. Spill it out. Tell me everything. Why you left, why you're back, and what the fuck you want from me. Everything. Let's get it over with."

She crossed her arms on her chest and glared at her. This conversation would be fruitless. She knew that. Melodie was obviously closed off to any justification she might have. Yet she was standing here in her room somewhat ready to listen, and Ana knew she wouldn't get another chance.

"Do you want to sit down?" she offered, indicating the bed with her hand.

"No. I want to hear you out so you can finally get out of my life for good. That's all I want. Is that clear?" Her pale blue eyes were fixed on her as if she could shoot icicles through her heart. Her body was fired up yet her stare and her words were glacial. Even the black pants and black V-neck sweater she wore beautifully helped make her message crystal clear. There was nothing open or receptive in her attitude and appearance. Nothing but austerity.

"Yes, very clear." At the risk of infuriating Melodie even more, she couldn't help but smile. She'd missed that fire in her. And anger was so much better than indifference. She stomped her foot, clicked her tongue and opened her eyes wider to communicate her impatience and command Ana to talk. "Okay then. I'll be quick. First of all I want to say I'm sorry. So sorry I left the way I did. And I came back because I was hoping you could forgive me, but I know now I had no right to." She paused and watched for a reaction, which she got in the form of an eye roll and a sigh. "I tried to explain to your father earlier and I realized I can't expect you to understand. I left because I couldn't stand being here. My grief over my mother's death got mixed up with my grief over Yvonne and I couldn't handle it. I had to get away so I could make sense of it all. But I know it was selfish, and I had no right to hope you could forgive me, so if all you want is to get rid of me, you don't even have to listen to another word. I've already decided I'll be leaving."

She swallowed, observed Melodie for any sign of softening on her part. All she saw was tears running down her face. Tears she didn't even try to wipe away, her arms still crossed on her chest. Ana grabbed the box of tissues on the nightstand and handed it to her. She shook her head. A single, sharp movement from left to right. "No. Don't try to comfort me. Just tell me why."

"Why I left? I already said…"

"No," she hissed with another movement of her head. "Why did you come back here hoping I would forgive you? It all comes back to the first question I asked you when you showed up here. What the hell are you doing here? What do you want, Ana?"

"Isn't that obvious?"

Melodie squared her jaw and shook her head again, daring her to speak. Ana then realized she hadn't told her the most important part of it all yet. To do so was putting herself in a vulnerable position, especially now that she was convinced she would be rejected, but she owed it to her.

"I wanted you to forgive me because I wanted to be here with you more than anything else. I wanted us to be a family. You, Thomas, and me. I love you, Melodie. I knew that even the day I left you alone with your father to mourn your grandmother. I knew I'd come back to you eventually, but I waited too long. I didn't tell you what was going on and I screwed up. I'll never forgive myself for losing you."

This time Melodie's tears were so abundant she was forced to wipe them away with her hands. "You could have said you needed time," she said with difficulty through sobs. "You could have answered my calls, or sent a text telling me you'd be back. I would have been pissed off but I would have waited."

"I know. At first I wasn't ready, and then I heard the desperation and anger when you left messages or sent texts, and I was a coward… Then you just stopped…" She moved closer to comfort her.

"No," Melodie hissed again before the stepped backward. "Stay away from me. It's too late now." Her eyes were red but dry and anger took over as she continued through clenched teeth, pointing her index finger at Ana to punctuate her tirade. "Do you know how long I've waited for you to come back? Hoping for a call or even a fucking email? Do you know how many articles about the storm and sea levels I've read, crying my eyes out thinking about you? Do you have any idea how many movies and TV shows use that stupid Canon in D tune you played the first time we kissed in their soundtrack?" She spoke louder and louder and stopped when tears threatened to fall for the second time. Ana was the one crying now, hating herself for hurting Melodie so deeply. What she'd done was unforgivable. "Do you have any fucking idea?" Melodie asked again, demanding a response.

"Yes," she simply said before she sat on the bed and used the tissues to blow her nose.

"Good," she replied, acting defiant, although Ana knew she was on the verge of breaking into tears again. "Now that we've both said what we had to say, all I have to add is that you're right. I can't forgive you and I want you out of here. Understood?"

"Yes. I just need a few days to find an apartment."

"An apartment? You're not going back to the States?"

"No," Ana said hesitantly. "I took a position at the UQAR. I'll be teaching at the university in Rimouski starting in January."

"Damn shit! You're kidding me, right?" Melodie yelled, throwing her arms in the air and letting them fall loudly to her hips. She clicked her tongue the way she did every time she was irritated and paced furiously in front of the bed.

"No, but Rimouski isn't that small. We might never see each other again. I'll try to make sure of that, don't worry."

"For fuck's sake, what's the matter with you?" she yelled again before she grunted and left the room, slamming the door behind her.

Ana lay on the bed with a grunt of her own. None of this conversation had gone as planned, but she wasn't surprised. All she felt was shame and self-hatred. She'd ruined everything, and there was no way she could make up for it. All she had left was her familiar retreat strategy, and she wondered if moving away from the sea could possibly hurt as much as giving up on the woman she loved. If it did, she finally understood the extent of the sacrifice she'd been asking people to make all these years. *You're a complete asshole, Ana Bloom.*

CHAPTER THIRTY-TWO

Melodie rolled on her side and pulled the duvet over her head. She'd gone to bed angry but woke up confused. It was so much easier to remain angry with Ana before she knew she wanted more than just to apologize and explain her actions. Before she knew she'd found a position in Rimouski and could be around all the time if she chose to forgive her. Before Ana declared that was what she wanted. To be here. Before she said she loved her. She grunted into her pillow and when that didn't suffice to express her level of frustration, she screamed. She couldn't forgive Ana. She couldn't trust her not to leave again.

"Are you all right?" she heard her father ask from the other side of her bedroom door.

"Yes, I'm fine. What time is it?"

"Six thirty."

"Oh shit. I'm up." She had to get dressed and hurry to work to start cooking before the Smiths came down for their last breakfast at the White Sheep Inn. It was Saturday so Ana would probably have eggs Benedict as well. She grabbed the first pair of clean jeans she could find and a grey pullover sweater sporting a loosely laced-up split neckline and placed them on the bed before she ran to the bathroom, almost crashing into her father in the hall.

"I'll have your coffee ready," he said as he stepped toward the kitchen.

"Thanks."

She locked herself inside the only bathroom in the duplex and grabbed a washcloth to clean her face. They'd thought about selling the place after her grandmother's death, but then she'd impulsively suggested that they could all live there together instead: her father, Thomas, and her. She'd desperately wanted to hang on to every piece of her grandmother that she could, and this house was a big part of her. So was her father. She'd almost regretted letting the idea out of her mouth when she'd imagined him coming home drunk every night and sharing her everyday space with a grown man she barely knew anymore, but she would have been wrong to change her mind.

Living with her father had turned out to be the best idea she'd ever had. Jerome had stopped drinking entirely, dedicating his life to her and Thomas. He often did small repairs at the inn, of course, but he also helped her with house chores. He played with Thomas and she enjoyed watching them interact. She glanced at the wooden stool he'd built and put under the bathroom vanity, saying it wouldn't be long before Thomas could use it to wash his own hands and brush his own teeth. When Melodie had argued that they needed to get him to use the toilet first, he'd laughed and scratched his beard before he concluded, "I'll leave that to you, I think."

She applied mascara to her eyelashes, brushed her hair, and rushed back to her bedroom to get dressed. She stopped in the kitchen to kiss her father on the cheek, and he handed her a travel mug with warm coffee. It was their routine, and it was comforting. Miller came to sit by her feet as he did every time she got ready to go out and she bent down to pet him. "Did he have his breakfast?"

"Yes. Did you talk to Ana?"

"Not yet," she lied as she put the travel mug down on the small round table to reach into the closet for her winter coat and boots. She put them on before she went back for Miller's leash and clipped it to his collar.

"How did it go?" he asked with a raised eyebrow.

She looked at him and sighed. She couldn't lie to him any more than she could lie to her grandmother. They read through her each and every time. "It went horribly and I don't want to talk about it. Come on, Miller. We're late for work." She grabbed the leash, her purse, and the travel mug and got out of the door before Jerome could follow up with another question.

Melodie made sure her eggs Benedict were under control on the stove before she went out to the dining room to serve coffee. The Smiths were sitting at their usual table and so was Ana. She quickly filled up all three cups and checked that there were enough milk, cream, and sugar on both tables before she went back to the kitchen. She'd hired a student during the summer to take in breakfast orders and handle service because there were too many guests for her to keep up by herself, but she did it all since the tourist season had ended. Next she would clean up the rooms and do laundry, another task she needed help with in the summer. The only way to keep busy during winter was to do everything herself. It was also the only way not to go broke.

She plated both eggs Benedict breakfasts and Mrs. Smith's croissant and jams and expertly carried all three plates to the dining room. "I think we'll eat it all up today. It's our last chance after all," Mr. Smith announced, attacking his plate as soon as it hit the table.

Melodie laughed. "Don't say that. You promised you'd be back this summer, remember?" She put Ana's plate in front of her without meeting her gaze. She'd managed to take in her order and serve her coffee without ever looking into her eyes and she planned on keeping it that way.

"Oh, I didn't forget. But that's a long time from now," Mr. Smith said before he took a second bite. She doubted he'd finish his meal, but she appreciated his eagerness.

"It'll go fast, you'll see."

She didn't wait for his reply before she went back to the kitchen and started on dishes. As much as she wanted to chat with the Smiths, actively ignoring Ana was too demanding at the moment. Her presence was too heavy and overpowering. She couldn't trust she'd be able to keep her composure if she stayed in the dining room any longer. When she went back to check on her guests a few minutes later, Ana was gone. She glanced at Miller's usual spot by the stairs and saw that he wasn't there. They were off for their daily walk. Melodie automatically took a deep breath, finding it easier to let the air fill her lungs now that it was not so saturated with Ana's being.

She walked to the Smiths' table, whose plates were almost empty, except for a couple of bites. "Wow, I'm impressed."

"It was delicious, darling. As always," Mrs. Smith complimented before she lightly tapped her husband's hand, who'd burped as discreetly as he could behind his napkin.

"Excuse me," he said, embarrassed.

She giggled and reassured him, "I take it as a compliment, sir. Please make sure to say goodbye before you leave," she added as she cleared their table.

"We will."

She smiled and left them to finish their coffee. She went to Ana's table and her heart tightened when she saw that she'd barely touched her meal. Ana was obviously suffering and although she didn't find pleasure in knowing she was hurting probably as much as she was, Melodie couldn't be the one to relieve that pain.

Ana walked faster than usual and made it to the church in less than fifteen minutes. When she walked with Yvonne, they usually went in the other direction, but if their daily stroll took them toward the church, they rarely made it there before Yvonne asked to turn around. Since her return, Ana had avoided going in Yvonne's preferred direction, the way that took them to the empty site of her family's beloved blue saltbox house. That entire side of the beach seemed empty now without Yvonne.

Once she was past the parking lot of the church and back on the beach, she unclipped Miller's leash and threw the ball for him again, but he stayed put by her side. She looked down at him and noticed he was panting. "Poor old man. Sorry, I'll slow down." She gave him water and resumed walking at a more leisurely pace. She realized she hadn't even glanced at the sea, focusing on every step she made away from the inn and Melodie. Now that all of her cards were on the table, being ignored by her hurt even worse than before. A part of Ana had hoped their talk might have softened Melodie's heart, but it seemed her confession had the opposite effect instead.

She turned to the frozen sea and didn't find comfort in its white, usually calming beauty. Its arid, dreary lack of color seemed hostile now. The icy snow under her feet made it difficult to keep her balance and the glacial air filling her lungs stung more than it appeased her. The wind violently hit her face and she concluded the placid winter could be as quietly brutal as Melodie. As if it was telling her she didn't belong. "I get it," she muttered.

As soon as she got back to the inn she headed upstairs, trying not to pay attention to Melodie exchanging hugs and kisses with the old couple that appeared to be checking out, judging by the luggage sitting in front of the reception desk. She envied the warm goodbyes. She then realized the couple's departure was one more reason to hurry and find a place to live. She couldn't be Melodie's only guest. It would be torture and she'd caused enough pain. Ana had never been one to overstay her welcome and she'd gone way past that line this time. Melodie was right. And so was the sea. She didn't belong here. Halfway up the stairs she turned back to glance at Miller, who stared at her but respected the invisible boundaries Yvonne had set for him. She smiled, thinking he'd be the only one who'd miss her, perhaps with Thomas. The dog finally lay down by the stairs and she continued to her room.

She started up her laptop and opened the email in which Professor Hubert listed sources where she could find ads for apartments to rent. She'd sold her house in Ithaca, but she wasn't ready to buy in Rimouski yet. She'd put all of her furniture in storage, figuring she'd rent for a year or two until she decided where she wanted to settle down. She'd hoped Melodie would be part of the house search at that time. That they'd work together to find and make their perfect home, but she had to let go of that dream now. She browsed the listings and noted the addresses and phone numbers of those that sounded most interesting on a piece of paper, keeping only the apartments that were available by January first or earlier.

Melodie helped the Smiths carry their luggage to their car and hurried back inside the inn to warm up after waving goodbye. Her plan was to clean their room and wash theirs and Ana's towels before she went home. She knew Ana wouldn't expect her to stay at the inn for her. She most likely didn't expect anything from her anymore. Melodie had made it clear she couldn't, and as Jerome had predicted, she seemed to respect that decision. She kept her distance, didn't try to talk to her, didn't even look at her. She'd given up. And although that's what Melodie wanted, she couldn't swallow that lump in her throat or chase away those damn threatening tears.

The entire time she cleaned the Smiths' room she hoped Ana would leave hers before she was forced to go knock on her door to ask if she had any towels to wash. Then as she turned off the vacuum cleaner she heard a door open and close and she thought her wish had been granted until she peeked in the hallway and saw towels sitting on the floor in front of room number one. Ana didn't want to see her. It was better that way, but it still hurt. She put away all of her cleaning supplies and placed all the used towels in a laundry basket. Instead of going straight to the basement, however, she stopped by the reception desk and grabbed Ana's article under the printer.

She loaded the industrial washer with all of the towels, added the detergent, and started the machine. Then she leaned against the north wall of the basement, close to the window, and started reading. There weren't any chairs in the basement, but she didn't want to get caught or be interrupted now that she'd finally decided to read "Living on the Edge."

The beginning of the article was exactly what she'd expected. Ana exposed why and how sea levels were rising and explained that it was too late to avoid them eventually flooding a large portion of the world's coastlines. Next she wrote about the retreat strategy and why it made more sense than any manmade protective measure. As she read that section, Melodie thought of the multiple fights they'd had over that subject, and she couldn't believe how much her own convictions had transformed in such a short period of time. The article was well written, but nothing new to Melodie, and she didn't understand why Ana had insisted she should read it soon after her return. Didn't she know she'd already convinced her moving away was the only solution?

But she understood when she got to the last part of the article, the one that introduced the people Ana called *the residents*. Melodie recognized her grandmother in the lady who walked her dog on the beach every day. The *twinkling light blue eyes* and *tender smile* could only be hers. She recognized herself in *the young business owner who claimed saltwater ran through her veins*. She recognized her family and her neighbors, who *worked together to fix everything the sea had broken during the storm without any rancor, as lovers recover from a bad fight that might have shattered a few dishes along the way*. She went on to explain that the ties between those *residents* and the sea were so strong that *it would be inhumane to propose a retreat strategy to such communities without offering them new ways to remain close to their beloved sea*.

Melodie took a deep breath and wiped away a few tears before she resumed reading. Ana recommended temporary, mobile structures that would be noninvasive but would allow coastline communities to keep some kind of proximity to the sea without risking their homes or their lives and without further weakening beaches that served as a natural protective barrier. Her ideas went from simple benches and picnic tables to more elaborate tiny houses that would be entirely off the grid and light enough to be pulled away quickly and easily when needed. The last sentence concluded that although the retreat strategy was the best solution, it needed to be adapted to each community. *Scientists and government officials need to plan what comes after any massive relocation with as much thought and care as they plan for the retreat itself, taking into consideration the fears and aspirations of these residents.*

Melodie rolled the article and placed it in the back pocket of her jeans while she moved the towels from the washer to the dryer. She couldn't help but smile. She'd expected Ana's article to be informative but dry. She was surprised to find so much empathy in it. Ana had shown great sensitivity and understanding and had offered practical solutions she could see her neighbors not only accept but support. She'd certainly inspired her and given her tons of ideas for what she might do with this land once the inn was relocated. Ideas she was dying to discuss with Ana. But she couldn't.

She went back upstairs and sat behind the reception desk, staring at the article. She found it difficult to resist the urge to run upstairs to talk to Ana, but she had to. They couldn't go back now. If Ana had shown her the same sensitivity after her grandmother's death as she'd shown in her writing, they probably wouldn't be in this position now, but they were. She couldn't change that. So she took a pen and wrote two words on the title page, then walked slowly upstairs and discreetly slid the paper under Ana's door. She heard steps coming toward the door, so she hurried back to the reception area, put on her winter coat and boots, and left.

She didn't drive straight to the duplex, however. She went to her grandmother's land up the hill instead. The one where she'd planned to move the inn. She hadn't come back to this place in a year, since her grandmother's death. She walked to the edge of the land with great difficulty, deep snow making each step laborious. When she arrived at the precipice, she stared at the view of the sea expanding in front of her and smiled. Although she was still heartbroken about what had happened with Ana, her writing had given her hope again. A project. Something to get excited about. That was more than reason enough to smile.

Ana recognized her paper on the floor as soon as she spotted the stubborn flared-up corner. She stood up, sighed, and dragged her feet toward the door to pick it up. Giving her article back was probably another way for Melodie to tell her she didn't want anything to do with her, and she really didn't need to be reminded of that again. She was already doing all she could to get out of the way as quickly as possible. She'd made appointments to see two apartments this afternoon and three more tomorrow. She would pick the best out of five and would be out in a few days. Yes, she could go to a different hotel in the meantime, but was that really necessary? Surely Melodie could tolerate her for a few more days, a few more walks with Miller, and a few more moments with Thomas.

As she got closer to the paper she noticed handwritten words on the title page and picked up her pace. She bent down to grab the article and smiled when she read the two words Melodie had written: *thank you.* She looked through every page for another note but wasn't surprised when she didn't find any. Those two words were enough. And writing them had probably been very difficult for Melodie. They proved she'd read her article and liked it. She wasn't foolish enough to think that meant she could forgive her, but perhaps they could part ways as friends, or at least not avoid each other for the rest of their lives. That was something, wasn't it?

CHAPTER THIRTY-THREE

Ana came back to the inn determined to call the owner of the last condo she'd seen and ask him to get the lease ready for her to sign. It was by far the best option. The two apartments she'd seen the day before reminded her too much of the inn with their Victorian charm. The first one she'd visited today was just as old without the charm and out of the two modern condos she'd seen afterward, the last won the prize thanks to its balcony and view of the sea. She'd be comfortable there. There was a pool and a gym in the building, not to mention an underground garage.

She walked inside the inn trying to ignore Melodie and Jerome sitting in the dining room, but she couldn't help but notice Melodie was crying. She paused long enough to offer a compassionate smile which Melodie returned as she listened to Jerome, who she guessed was trying to comfort her even though she couldn't understand what he was saying in French. She waited for Jerome to stop talking and announced, hoping it would cheer her up, "I found a place. I'll be checking out on New Year's Eve."

"Oh, that's good," she replied before she cried harder and Jerome took her in her arms.

So much for cheering her up, Ana thought as she watched, powerless. "It's what you want, isn't it?"

"Yes," she hissed. "Don't flatter yourself; these tears have nothing to do with you. You don't have exclusive ownership of my tears, you know. Now go, please. Leave us alone." She waved her hand dismissively before she hid her face against Jerome's chest. Ana climbed the stairs slowly, still wanting nothing more than to find out what was troubling Melodie so much and comfort her, but understanding she'd lost that privilege.

"That was harsh," Jerome said once Ana had disappeared upstairs.

"I know," Melodie admitted as she pulled away from her father's embrace and dried her tears with a tissue he'd handed her earlier. He was right. It wasn't Ana's fault her mother had texted that she'd be at the inn for a few days during the holidays to spend time with her and Thomas.

"She'd probably understand what you're going through better than anyone, baby. From what I understand she didn't have the best relationship with her own mother. That's what got her so messed up she had to leave last year."

"I know," she repeated.

"She hurt you, and it's up to you if you want to forgive her or not. But it doesn't give you the right to treat her like shit."

"I know, I know, all right?" she stood up and clicked her tongue, exasperated by the way her father defended Ana but mostly annoyed with her own behavior. It was too easy to use Ana as a scapegoat for all of her frustrations. She took a deep breath before she added, "I'll apologize to her, okay?"

Jerome nodded and stood up. "Are you coming home now? I'll make dinner."

"No, I asked Kevin to drop off Thomas here when he called earlier. But you go ahead. We'll be home for dinner. What are you making?"

"Cereal," he said with a grin and a wink. She couldn't help but giggle. "I'll throw in an omelette if you smile." She did before he added more seriously, "You're gonna be all right?"

"Yes," she said with another weak smile. He kissed her forehead, winked at her again and left. She stood in the lobby, staring at the door her father had closed behind him, lost in thoughts about her mother until she heard steps behind her. She turned and came face to face with Ana.

"Sorry, I'll leave you alone, I promise. I was on my way out to grab a bite to eat," she said, avoiding her gaze as she walked past her.

"Wait, Ana," she started. Her heart tightened when she saw the tall, strong scientist turn around looking like a lost child expecting to be scolded. Her father was right. She had no right to keep torturing her despite all the pain she'd gone through when she'd left. They'd talked, she'd asked her to leave, and Ana was respecting that decision. What more did she want? Except for none of it to have happened in the first place. "I'm sorry about what I said before. I was upset because my mother is coming to the inn for the holidays. It had nothing to do with you and I shouldn't have barked at you like that."

"Don't worry about it. Are you okay?"

"Not really," she admitted as she smiled to avoid crying. "I don't know how to be around her, you know? It's like I don't even know her anymore."

"That could be the best thing about this whole situation."

"What do you mean?" Ana took a step toward her and she didn't back away, curious to find out how not knowing the woman her mother had become could be positive.

"I'm guessing she wants to meet her grandson, right?" She nodded. "Then the question is: do you want Thomas to meet his grandmother and get to know her?"

"Yes, otherwise I would have told her to go to hell. I do want my son to know all of his family, but I'm scared to death of what seeing her will do to me."

"Understandably so. But do you want to know what I think?"

"I'm listening, aren't I?" She sighed with impatience as Ana took off her winter jacket and sat on the bottom step of the stairs. Miller joined her and she petted him. Melodie placed her hands on her hips and prompted, "Well, tell me."

"I think you need to mourn the person you knew as your mother to make room for the woman you don't know who's about to visit."

"What? She's not dead. What the hell are you talking about?"

"But in a way she is, isn't she? What's your mother's name?"

"Nicole," she replied as she joined Ana on the step.

"Nicole isn't your mother. She hasn't been the mother you needed her to be ever since she abandoned you here with your father when you were fourteen. Are you with me so far?"

"Yes," she said as she crossed her arms on her chest, a chill passing through her body as she heard the words come out of Ana's mouth. She was right. The mother she'd known had died when she'd moved to Montreal. Ana put her arm around Melodie and rubbed her arm slowly. The thought of pulling away crossed her mind, but she needed this comforting touch too much to move.

"You need to let go of that woman who was your mother if you want to make room for Nicole."

"And how the fuck do I do that?" she asked as she let her head fall onto Ana's shoulder.

"Make your peace with her. Take the time to remember all the good times you had together, and then forgive her. Let her go." Ana's voice broke as she spoke softly, whispering almost directly into her ear, and she realized she knew exactly what she was talking about.

"That's what you did, isn't it? When you left the hospital and went back to Ithaca last year?"

"Yeah."

By the time she'd made it to Ithaca last January, Ana had spent the long drive remembering all the reasons why Constance had no right to interfere with her happiness now, to keep haunting her the way she did. She'd driven straight to her grave. Angry, she'd yelled out her long list of grievances, thinking it would free her from her mother's hold at last. But it had only left her angrier. After days of wallowing in resentment, unable to make sense of anything, she'd finally decided to ask for help. It took months of therapy before she understood forgiveness was the better option, so she didn't expect Melodie to believe her, yet she hoped sharing her own experience might help.

"I can't forgive her, Ana. She hurt me too much."

"I know. That's what I thought too. It took months. That's why I didn't come back before. But eventually I started thinking of the good times I had with her. I thought of the places we visited together across the country. The way she laughed. How important I felt when I helped her learn her lines. My pride when I saw her on stage. I focused on those little things instead of her bigger shortcomings I'd let take over my life. And I forgave her."

"And it worked? It made you feel better?"

"I wouldn't be here if it hadn't worked. Don't get me wrong, the bad memories and the bitterness still flare up once in a while, but when they do I start thinking of the better days, and I forgive her all over again. Forgiving her freed me to move on and allow myself to be happy. I know it sounds silly, but what they say about forgiveness is true."

"What is that?" she asked as she turned to look into her eyes.

"Ultimately you do it for you. Not for the person who hurt you."

Melodie looked pensive for a few seconds before she shook her head. "I can't."

"I understand," she said as she dared moving a few curls out of Melodie's face with her fingers.

"You're a bigger person than I am."

"No. I spent a fortune in therapy, that's all."

Melodie laughed and she smiled wider than she had in over a year. Ana had thought she'd never know that pleasure again—being the cause of that beautiful, explosive laughter she'd missed so much. Their eyes remained locked onto each other even as Melodie stopped laughing. She saw her expression change and sadness settled in her eyes before she averted her gaze and stood, putting some distance between them. She wasn't ready to forgive her any more than she was ready to forgive her mother. "Well, I guess I'll go grab some food."

"Oh yes, of course. Don't let me keep you any longer." She petted Miller one last time and made her way to the door before she heard Melodie's voice again, "Thank you, Ana."

"Anytime," she replied as she opened the door and faced the frigid winter. She ran to her car remembering how Yvonne had once told her she was good at planting seeds in people's minds. She hoped she'd done exactly that today. For Melodie's sake.

CHAPTER THIRTY-FOUR

Melodie used Scotch tape to hang a shimmering gold garland from one side of the reception desk to the other. She hadn't planned on decorating the inn for the holidays, but a young couple had just booked a reservation for the day after Christmas so she figured she had to show some kind of holiday spirit. Thomas seemed fascinated with the simple decoration, clapping enthusiastically when she stepped away from the desk to assess her handiwork. She picked him up and kissed him on the cheek. "You like it, huh?" He clapped again and she laughed, inspired by his excitement.

She usually got passionate about everything around the holiday season, from decorating to cooking. But this would be their first Christmas without her grandmother, not to mention that Nicole would show up any day now. She'd practiced referring to her as Nicole instead of her mother. She'd spent the last two days pondering Ana's words, and although she wasn't any closer to forgiving her, imagining her as a stranger named Nicole instead of the mother who'd abandoned her strangely helped her perspective.

She'd tried thinking of the good times like Ana had suggested, but they were buried so deeply that she had a hard time finding any. She'd finally been able to dig up a vague image of her mother making homemade playdough with flour, water, food coloring, and a few other ingredients she couldn't remember. They would spend hours modelling different animals and characters. As the image became clearer, she remembered laughing so hard her belly hurt. And she was reminded of how much she'd loved hearing her mother laugh. Her laughter was not like hers and her father's. It was quieter, closer to a wheezing sound punctuated with an occasional snorting that made her laugh even more.

"That looks good," Ana declared as she came down the stairs, startling her. "I figured you wouldn't be decorating."

"I didn't think I would either, but why not?" She turned to face her. "Are you going for a walk?" she asked when she noticed Ana was wearing her Merrell boots and winter jacket.

"Yes, would you like to join me?"

"If you don't mind walking on the street. The beach is a little tough with the stroller."

"Sure, I think Miller and I can manage the street today," Ana said with a mischievous grin.

Melodie smiled as she rolled her eyes. "All right, will you help me get Thomas dressed?"

"Of course."

They'd been cordial to each other since their talk about Nicole and forgiveness. Melodie wasn't sure how long this truce would last, but she purposefully avoided talking about the relationship they'd almost had or the pain she'd gone through in the last twelve months. She didn't want to ruin this detente. She needed Ana's friendship right now. She needed her support and her advice much more than her anger. Perhaps knowing she would leave the inn in a few days helped her see things differently, although her stomach turned into knots every time she thought about it.

As they stepped outside and she installed Thomas in his stroller, she realized that although they'd both taken daily walks for as long as they'd known each other, this would be the first time they walked together.

They started in the direction of the church without hesitation, as if it was the only way to go. She pushed the stroller and Ana held on to Miller's leash. "Have you signed your lease yet?"

"Yes. The tenant will be out between Christmas and New Year's so all I'll need to do is clean up and move in."

"Don't you need to go get your furniture in Ithaca? Or buy some?"

"No, it's furnished."

"Oh, well that's convenient." She heard the lack of sincerity in her own voice. She didn't understand the weight in her chest, the panic at the thought of Ana leaving the White Sheep Inn.

"Do you know when Nicole will be arriving?"

The heaviness in her chest multiplied instantly at Ana's question, and she understood that more than anything she was terrified of being left alone with the woman she desperately tried not to think of as her mother.

"Any day now, I guess."

"If you want, I can wait until she goes back to Montreal before I move out," Ana suggested. "I mean, if you think that would be helpful," she added hesitantly.

Melodie sighed with relief and grabbed Ana's arm. "That would be so helpful. You have no clue."

"Great. I'll stay then."

"Thank you."

"There's no need to thank me, Melodie. I'll stay as long as you need me. The only reason I'm leaving is because you asked me to."

"Right," she simply said, avoiding meeting her gaze. Saying anything else would bring them back to the reasons why she'd asked Ana to leave and would disturb their newfound and fragile peace. Besides, she wasn't sure what she could say next. She couldn't ask her to stay, could she? Things would eventually get too complicated if she did. "It's cold, huh?"

"Yes," Ana replied softly with a hint of sadness.

They walked in silence the rest of the way to the church. Although silence between them had once been comfortable, it was now awkward and she felt obligated to break it when they turned around to go back to the inn. "When are you starting your new job?"

"Second week of January."

"You must have made a great impression on them when you were conducting your interviews. I mean for them to offer you a position like that. It's pretty impressive."

"It didn't really happen that way. They didn't just offer me a position. I had to convince them I was worth it. It wasn't easy but fortunately Professor Hubert supported me and together we showed the ISMER team I would be a valuable asset to the institute."

"What team?"

"ISMER. *Institut des Sciences de la Mer de Rimouski.* Don't make fun of my accent. I'll learn eventually."

She couldn't help but smile, but not because she was making fun of Ana. She actually found her accent adorable. "I won't, and I'm sure you will. I've heard of the Institute of Marine Science. I'm sure you have a lot to bring to their team."

"Yes, well, some would argue the pay cut I took didn't quite make sense for my career, but I wanted to be here more than anything."

"Oh, Ana, I'm so sorry." She shouldn't feel guilty. She hadn't asked Ana to give up her job to move to Rimouski, yet she couldn't help but feel somewhat responsible.

"Don't be. I don't regret anything," she quickly said to reassure her. "Apart from leaving in the first place, of course."

And there they were again. Perhaps a walk was a little too much time together to avoid picking at wounds that hadn't properly healed yet. As they approached the inn, Melodie was relieved to find a new car in the parking lot. Welcoming a new guest to the inn would successfully distract her from the awkwardness of her walk with Ana, she thought, as she hurried inside, carrying Thomas in her arms. Her relief was short-lived, however, and immediately replaced with unbearable anxiety when she recognized the new guest standing in the lobby.

"Hi, Melodie."

"Hi, Nicole," she replied in a barely audible voice, grateful for the strong hand she felt on her lower back.

"And this is Thomas, I suppose? Oh he's so precious," she continued as she moved toward them, stopping only when Melodie instinctively stepped backward into Ana's arms. "And you are?" she asked as she looked over her shoulder at Ana.

Nicole spoke French but Ana understood she was asking for her name when she looked at her. "Ana Bloom. Nice to meet you," Ana answered as she stepped around Melodie to shake the woman's hand. Nicole was strikingly beautiful and elegant. She'd obviously given Melodie her round face and dimples, but her eyes were dark brown and her hair was straight, although Ana suspected she might have straightened it. It was too perfect, smooth and shiny, and the red color was clearly artificial. Her dark green suit had the perfect fit and her handshake was firm but not overpowering. Everything about her screamed business, from her polished appearance to the polite arrogance in her half smile.

"Nice to meet you, Ana," she answered in English with barely a hint of an accent. Several questions passed through her eyes, but Ana was grateful she didn't dare voice any of them. Ana wouldn't have been able to explain her role or place in Melodie's life at the moment, and she was certain Melodie didn't want to explain either, as she moved away from them to sit Thomas on the reception desk and undress him, "Oh, could I please do it?" Nicole asked in a small voice, going from strong business woman to scared and tentative in a second.

"Sure," Melodie granted. She stepped back to give Nicole enough room and Ana grabbed her hand. She meant it as a brief show of encouragement but Melodie squeezed her hand tightly and wouldn't let go. They watched in silence as Nicole undressed Thomas, who smiled and laughed at the funny faces and voices she made for his entertainment.

"He laughs exactly like you did at that age. I couldn't get enough of that sound," she said as she turned to them. Her smile appeared genuine and her eyes glistened with tears. She looked at their joined hands and dared to ask at last, "Are you two together?" Melodie dropped Ana's hand and they looked at each other, panicked. "It's fine if you are. I know you're gay, Melodie," she added, misunderstanding their hesitation to answer.

"And how the hell would you know that?" Melodie hissed between clenched teeth before she pushed Nicole away from Thomas and finished taking off his snowsuit.

Nicole closed her eyes and sighed. "I know more than you think. You're my daughter, after all."

Melodie picked up Thomas and handed him to Ana before she turned back to Nicole. "No. I was your daughter a very long time ago. We're nothing but strangers now and my love life is none of your business. The only reason I let you come here was to give you a chance not to be a stranger to your grandson too. Is that clear?" Nicole nodded sheepishly. "Now if you'll follow me, I'll show you to your room." She grabbed a key from behind the reception desk and headed upstairs. Nicole took her suitcase and followed.

Ana put Thomas down on the floor and took off her winter jacket and boots before she got on her knees to join him in petting Miller. "I think he's thirsty. Do you want to come with me and get water for him?" Thomas nodded and she took his hand to lead him toward the kitchen. Before they'd made it out of the lobby, however, Melodie came back downstairs, took off her jacket and placed it on its usual hook. "Are you okay?" Ana asked.

"Not really," she said as calmly as she could, as if she could burst into tears at any moment. "I promised myself I wouldn't let her upset me and I couldn't even last two minutes. I didn't want her to think she can still affect me, damn shit." She hit the reception desk with her fist and Thomas jumped, startled.

Ana handed him his favorite stuffed animal before she moved closer to Melodie and rubbed her back gently.

"You must think I didn't listen to a word you said the other day, but I did. I'm really trying," Melodie said before her voice broke and she started sobbing. She turned and Ana welcomed her in her arms. She rocked her gently as she caressed her hair.

"I don't think anything of the sort. I didn't talk to you about my own mother to dictate what you should do with yours. The last thing you should worry about is what I think, but I'm actually proud of what you did."

"Really? You don't think I was unfair?" she asked against her shoulder as the sobs subsided.

"Absolutely not. You set your limits, and there's nothing wrong with that. And you're giving her the opportunity to become a real grandmother to Thomas, despite your own feelings about her. That's so generous. I truly admire you for that."

"Really?" she repeated as she broke their embrace to look at her.

"Really." She couldn't resist caressing her face and was surprised when Melodie leaned into her hand. "You're amazing, don't you know that? And certainly the best mother I've ever met in my life."

Melodie smiled and placed a soft kiss in the palm of her hand before she answered, "Thank you. For this and for earlier. For being here with me."

"I've told you before. I'll be here for you as long as you let me." Melodie's gaze dropped, and she appeared as uncomfortable as the first time she'd said those words during their walk. Resigned, Ana stepped away to give her space. "I'll go get water for Miller," she announced before she left the lobby. She was convinced a part of Melodie wanted to ask her to stay, but she respected the bigger part of her that didn't trust her. She'd be here to support her while she needed it, but she'd leave as soon as Nicole did, as promised.

CHAPTER THIRTY-FIVE

Melodie placed doughnuts in a large serving plate and sprinkled a pinch of powdered sugar on top. She slightly opened the kitchen door and glanced into the dining room where they'd put two tables together to seat Nicole, Kevin, Ana, Jerome, Thomas and herself. She watched as Nicole amused Thomas with crayons at one end of the table while Jerome and Kevin argued about hockey at the other end. Ana sat in the middle and when she saw Melodie look in her direction, she realized she'd been caught and immediately closed the kitchen door.

She placed a white paper filter in the coffee machine and filled the coffeepot with cold water, taking her time to return to the dining room. Nicole had been at the inn for three days and tonight was her last night. After dinner, Kevin would be taking Thomas to spend a few days with his family so there was no reason for her to stay any longer. Nicole seemed to accept that although Melodie welcomed her presence for Thomas's sake, she didn't want to be alone with her. Since she'd made her limits clear at her arrival, Nicole hadn't attempted to show interest in her life or to start up any type of conversation. She respected her boundaries, and Melodie was grateful for that.

Still, tonight was Christmas Eve and she'd decided to make it a special night, some kind of celebration, despite her imperfect family and her lack of motivation. She'd made the effort for Thomas, she repeated to herself. She'd cooked turkey with all the trimmings and she'd made homemade doughnuts, a recipe she'd learned from her father, who'd inherited it from her great-grandmother. She stared at the glass pot as coffee slowly dripped into it.

"This looks delicious. Can I help with anything?" Ana asked as she entered the kitchen and eyed the plated dessert.

"You can take this plate to the table. I'll join you with the coffee as soon as it's ready."

Instead of leaving the kitchen with the dessert as instructed right away, Ana put her arm around her shoulders and squeezed gently. She'd been so attentive for the last three days, always there to check on Melodie and to show her support, whether it was with an encouraging touch like this one or simple eye contact that reminded Melodie she was on her side. Melodie was quickly growing used to her presence. She counted on it. Perhaps a little too much. She didn't want to put herself in a position where she relied on Ana, yet that's exactly what she'd done. "Are you okay?"

"Yeah, thanks. Go ahead, I'll be there in a minute."

"All right."

Ana left with the plate of doughnuts and Melodie watched Nicole's reaction from the door. She saw her smile and put a hand to her heart before she looked up and spotted her. Her eyes shimmered with tears, and she smiled before she closed the kitchen door again. She'd made Nicole's favorite dessert on purpose, although she couldn't explain why. The reason she was staying in the kitchen for so long was not because she couldn't stand sitting at a table with Nicole or even being in the same room with her, as she'd let her father, Kevin, and even Ana believe. The real reason was much worse.

The more time she spent in Nicole's presence and the more she watched her play and exchange with Thomas, the more good memories came back to her. She remembered laughing at the same grimaces Thomas found so hilarious. She remembered the bedtime stories she heard her tell Thomas at night before they went back to the duplex and left her alone at the inn with Ana. When she watched her draw with Thomas, she remembered the hours they spent drawing together, making up stories as they went. Nicole was a talented artist and each of their stories was like an improvised comic book Melodie kept with such pride until her mother moved away. She'd looked for them at the duplex, hoping her grandmother had kept them, but she figured they'd probably been destroyed inside the blue saltbox house in the storm of 2010. Then, as she was deciding on the menu for tonight's dinner, she remembered how much her mother loved these doughnuts and how her father used to make them every year for Christmas. The good times were flooding her mind, and she didn't know what to do with them.

She took a deep breath, retrieved the full coffeepot, and finally headed back to the dining room, where everyone waited for her. "Go ahead, help yourselves while I serve the coffee." Her guests didn't need more convincing to grab a doughnut, and she couldn't help but watch Nicole bite into hers as she poured coffee for her father.

"Oh, Melodie, these are divine," she declared as she looked into her eyes.

"Thank you," she replied with a smile before she averted her eyes, unable to keep her heart from being filled with pride.

"They're really good, baby. Even better than mine," her father added. "I stopped making these years ago. If I'd known you still had the recipe I would have asked you to make them all the time," he said before he exploded in laughter.

Melodie silently cussed her father for letting the cat out of the bag. She didn't want Nicole to think she'd made the dessert especially for her, but it was too late now. As she turned to watch her reaction she saw her mouth the words "thank you," and Melodie looked away without acknowledging her gratitude. *Damn shit, Dad, couldn't you keep your mouth shut?*

They enjoyed dessert and coffee before Kevin discreetly announced they'd better leave for his parents' house before Thomas's bedtime. "I'll help Melodie with the dishes and I'll be on my way as well," Nicole added to everyone's surprise, including Melodie's.

"You don't have to drive to Montreal this late. Stay the night," she offered.

"Don't worry. I'll be fine. I have friends in Quebec City I can stay with if I don't feel like going all the way home. Besides, we had a deal, didn't we?" She smiled and Melodie smiled back, grateful for her understanding. "I hope I can come back soon, though. I really do want to spend more time with my grandson."

"Of course. All you have to do is let me know and I'll have a room ready for you."

"Thank you." Melodie nodded and Nicole smiled again before she stood up and started clearing the table.

"Please, leave that. If you're going to get on the road tonight, go ahead and get your things from your room. I'll handle the dishes."

"Are you sure?"

"Absolutely."

"I'll help," Ana added. She didn't waste any time and started clearing the table as Melodie went to get Thomas's bag and handed it to Kevin. Nicole kissed Thomas goodbye and promised to visit again soon. Melodie put on her winter jacket and followed Kevin and Thomas outside.

"She seems genuine about wanting to be part of his life," Kevin conceded as he secured Thomas into his car seat.

"Yeah, I know, but it's weird, don't you think? I mean, why now?"

Kevin closed the door and shrugged. "Maybe it took her that long to get the guts to face you again," he suggested before he walked around the SUV and opened the driver's door. "Merry Christmas, Mel."

"Merry Christmas," she almost whispered as she considered his theory. It made sense. Perhaps Nicole's shame was what had kept her away from Thomas for the first eighteen months of his life. She liked that idea. It was comforting. It made her more human than the selfish monster she'd imagined until now.

She watched the SUV leave the parking lot, and before she could go back inside, Nicole came out the door, dragging her suitcase behind her. She stopped to face Melodie. "Thank you for your hospitality. And Merry Christmas," she said awkwardly, making a move as if to hug her before she stopped herself.

"Merry Christmas," Melodie repeated with a hesitant smile. Nicole walked to her car and put her suitcase in the trunk, but Melodie couldn't let her drive away yet. "Nicole?"

"Yes?" She turned, a hopeful smile on her face.

"Do you still have that recipe for homemade playdough you used to make?"

Nicole's smile widened and she nodded with enthusiasm. "Yes, of course. Would you like to have it?"

"Yeah, I would if you don't mind."

"I'll email it to you as soon as I get back home."

"Thank you."

"No. Thank you."

"Drive safely."

Nicole nodded again, got into her car and drove away.

CHAPTER THIRTY-SIX

When she went back inside, her father was in the lobby, putting on his jacket. "Are you leaving too?"

"Yes, I tried to help with the dishes but Ana shooed me away. I'm a little tired, baby. This was a weird dinner for me."

"Oh, I know, Dad. Thank you so much for being there for me." She hugged him to show her gratitude.

"You know I can't say no to you. And I'm not the only one," he added as he jerked his chin toward the kitchen.

"She's been pretty awesome. I'll be the first to admit that." She couldn't help the grin on her face as she thought of Ana's generous presence by her side through the past few days.

"How are you doing? I bet you're glad Nicole is gone, huh?"

"Yes, but it wasn't as bad as I thought. Her visit really messed with my mind, but she's good with Thomas, so I'm a little torn to say the least."

The wrinkles on the sides of his eyes deepened and she knew he was smiling before his lips twitch through his beard. "And you're torn about Ana too, aren't you?" She closed her eyes and clicked her tongue. She didn't know how to answer that question. Torn didn't seem strong enough of a word to describe how she felt about Ana right now. "You don't have to answer," her father continued. "I can see it. I understand she hurt you, but you know, sometimes the only people we punish by holding on to grudges are ourselves. Think about that, okay?"

"Yeah, I haven't been thinking about much else for the past few days, to tell you the truth."

He kissed her forehead and sighed. "Sometimes I think you've had to forgive my mistakes so many times you've used up all of your mercy on me, and I wonder if I was worth it. I've let you down over and over again. I've hurt you over and over again. Yet I've never lost your love or your trust. Why is that, baby? Why aren't you angry with me like you are with your mother or with Ana?"

"I've wondered about that lately and you know what? I think in the end I could never stay mad at you because I always knew where to find you. You were always there, at least physically. If you weren't home, you were at the bar. I couldn't depend on you for anything, but you were here in your own way. Nicole and Ana, they left me, Dad. I didn't know where to find them anymore." She started crying and her father held her until she stopped, swaying gently from left to right.

"I don't think this one is going anywhere now," he whispered. "Don't keep punishing yourself uselessly." He kissed the top of her head and added with a wink, "Go on now, and don't let her do all those dishes alone."

He left and she joined Ana in the kitchen, observing her from the doorway. She was standing at the sink, washing pots and pans. She'd taken off her sweater and the sleeves of her light green shirt were rolled up to her elbows. Melodie smiled. She believed her father. Chances were Ana wouldn't be leaving again. She might not be able to trust it completely yet but she believed it. She didn't have the strength to keep that grudge alive any longer on the off chance she did leave again. She'd had enough. It made no sense for her to put any more energy on trying to keep up this animosity she didn't really feel anymore.

For what? Out of pride? Out of fear? She was done punishing herself. She may not be ready to forgive her mother yet, and she would have to keep working on it during each of her future visits, but that's where she would put her energy from now on. She grabbed a dish towel to dry the pots and pans Ana had placed on a rack by the sink.

"So is everyone gone now?"

"Mhm," she confirmed.

"And how do you feel?"

"Hopeful is the best word to describe it, I think."

"That's good." She paused before she added, "I'll be out of here tomorrow. I got the keys to the condo earlier today, so I'll go clean up in the morning."

"Okay," she said, unable to keep the sadness out of her voice.

Ana glanced at her, perplexed. "That was our deal, right? I stayed to offer you support while Nicole was here, but you still want me to move out, right?"

"I guess, yes. I mean, you can't stay in a hotel for the rest of your life."

"Well, no, I can't. But that's not the reason why I'm leaving. You asked me to leave, remember?"

"Yes."

"Then why do you sound so sad? You're confusing the hell out of me right now."

"I'm sad because I'll miss you. But I don't think it'd be wise to start living together so soon."

Ana dropped the large pot she was scrubbing and soapy water splattered all over the front of her shirt. She turned to face Melodie. "What are you talking about?"

"I'm talking about us. I think it will be good for you to have your own place, at least for a while. I can see you at the condo, and you can see me at the duplex, like people do."

"What people?"

She grinned and chuckled before she answered. It wasn't every day she saw her confident scientist this disoriented, and she had fun with it. "People as in couples, silly."

"Couples? Melodie, are you saying you want us to date? Are you saying you're ready to forgive me?"

Her voice was shaking, hopeful but frightened at the same time. Melodie moved closer and plunged her hands into her thick, messy hair. She'd been dying to do this since Ana had come back into her life. "Yes," she finally answered. "But I'm not doing it for you. I'm doing it for me," she added before she pulled Ana to her and pressed their lips together.

Over the months Ana had been gone Melodie had slowly convinced herself her lips had never been as soft as she remembered them. Her kisses had never been as sensual and arousing as she remembered either. It only took one taste of her mouth to realize she'd been wrong not to trust her memory. Ana's kisses were perfect. So were her hands, strong and firm against her butt as she lifted her onto the countertop. She wrapped her legs around Ana's waist and pulled her bottom lip into her mouth. She broke the kiss to catch her breath and leaned her head backward to offer her neck and her chest, left exposed by a plunging V-neck sweater. She expected Ana to accept her invitation to explore the nude flesh with her lips but instead Ana asked, "Are you sure about this?"

She looked at Ana then, examined her expression. Her pupils were dilated, her breathing was ragged, her mouth open. She undeniably wanted her. Although she was politely asking permission, her body was warning her that this was her last chance to turn back. All Melodie had to do was say yes to unleash a desire that wouldn't be bottled up anymore. So she did. Without a word. She took off her sweater and pulled Ana closer with her legs first, crushing her against her sex before she pulled her face to her breasts, giving her the most intimate parts of her in a yes that couldn't be misinterpreted.

Ana took everything she offered with greedy hands and a ravenous mouth. Her eagerness was almost painful at times, but Melodie still wanted more. They'd shared only one night before and they'd spent a year wanting it back. They were making love with all of that pent-up energy now. It couldn't be gentle, thoughtful, or controlled in any way. It was raw, untamed, and desperate. Ana moved her bra out of her way to take a nipple into her mouth. She sucked it hard as she unbuttoned her pants and slid a hand into abundant wetness. She knew it wouldn't take much for her to come. Every nerve in her was turned on and ready to explode, yet she didn't want to come alone. She needed to pleasure Ana.

"Get on the floor," she commanded as she pushed herself off the counter. Ana obeyed and they both stripped out of their pants and panties before Melodie lay on top of her, her face hovering above Ana's sex as Melodie's hovered above Ana's mouth, breathing her in before she plunged her mouth and her tongue into her folds, devouring her clumsily as Ana did the same to her. They didn't need languorous precision now. Within a few minutes she reached what resembled release more than climax, closely followed by Ana.

She turned around and kissed Ana's mouth before she lay on top of her, her face on her heaving chest. Their breathing synchronized and slowed together, until Ana was finally able to speak. "I don't think this is how dating works," she said with a low chuckle.

Melodie laughed before she replied, "Too bad. I was thinking we could take this to your room, but we probably shouldn't."

"No, we probably shouldn't. On the other hand, I've always wondered how loud that bed could squeak."

They laughed together and waited until they fully caught their breath before they stood, gathered their clothes, and moved upstairs to room number one, where they made love with less urgency, more tenderness, but with as much longing as they had in the kitchen.

CHAPTER THIRTY-SEVEN

Ana had feared the condo would be the saddest place where she'd ever lived. She'd thought she would come to its modern design and furniture to live alone and lonely, isolated from Melodie, Thomas, Miller, Jerome, all of those she'd come to think as family. Instead, Melodie had come with her this morning, armed with a mop, a bucket, and plenty of cleaning supplies. They'd scrubbed the one-bedroom apartment from top to bottom, and then they'd tried its large glass and ceramic shower together before they'd thoroughly tested the king-size bed. She didn't doubt she'd be happy in this condo now, as she sipped on coffee, sitting at the small dining table with Melodie and enjoying the view outside the oversized patio door that led to the balcony. She wasn't sure what had pushed Melodie over the edge, what had made her decide to give her another chance, but she was certain she wouldn't mess it up this time.

"This balcony will be the place to be this summer," Melodie said with enthusiasm. "It's large enough for a table and a couple of chairs. Maybe even a hammock."

"That sounds lovely," she agreed as she entwined their fingers on the tabletop.

"A scientist once told me I should learn to appreciate the sea from a distance. This is probably what she had in mind." She winked and Ana chuckled. She'd missed this free, playful side of Melodie.

"It's definitely one of them. That scientist sounds pretty smart."

"She is. But she's also gorgeous," she added as she walked around the table and sat on her lap to tousle her curls. "She has this amazing hair I can't stay away from and beautiful green eyes that remind me of the sea."

"But you don't have to admire them from a distance."

"Thank god, because she also has soft lips I can't resist kissing," she replied before she brushed her lips against Ana's. She deepened the kiss enough to awaken every fiber in Ana's body, and then stopped, leaving her wanting so much more. "I love you," she whispered against her quivering mouth.

The words sharpened her arousal even further and she practically begged Melodie, "Let me take you back to bed." She complemented her proposal with a series of soft kisses on Melodie's neck, aware of their effect. She felt the vibration of her moan on her lips as it passed through her throat, and she thought her plea would be granted until Melodie's sensual tremors were replaced with contradicting words.

"Absolutely. We'll go back to bed, but not right now. I want to show you something first." She planted one last chaste kiss on Ana's lips and jumped up from her lap.

"Are you kidding me?" Ana protested, unable to hide her disappointment.

"Nope. Come on, get dressed. The faster we get there, the sooner we'll be back in your gigantic bed." She didn't wait for Ana's answer before she ran to the bedroom.

"We have to go out in this cold?" She griped dramatically, unwilling to give up the comfort of her condo and Melodie's company. She dragged her feet to the bedroom where Melodie was already buttoning up her jeans.

"Yes. And we might even need snowshoes. Do you have any? We'll have to stop by the duplex to get mine, and if you don't have any, we can borrow my father's."

"I have snowshoes, but I wasn't planning on using them today," she objected. "Where are we going?"

"It's a surprise. And quit complaining. I promise you'll love it. Now get moving." She playfully slapped Ana's behind before she put on her sweater. Resigned and growing more curious, Ana got dressed. There was no point arguing anyway. She'd follow Melodie anywhere.

Melodie struggled to keep up with Ana as they walked toward the edge of the cliff. As she suspected, they needed snowshoes to walk in the deep virgin snow that covered the entire property. Even the marks she'd left during her last visit had disappeared under fresh snow and walking without snowshoes would have been more than laborious this time around. Ana suddenly stopped, and from the way she gasped, Melodie knew they'd reached their destination. They took in the view that left Ana speechless, her mouth wide open. The frozen sea was at their feet, at the bottom of the hill, behind the church and colorful houses that could only enhance the view from this angle. White mixed with grey and blue, and she couldn't be sure where the sea ended and the sky began. The glacial wind was brutal, but Melodie smiled nonetheless. "What do you think?"

"It's breathtaking. Is this what I think it is?"

"Yes. We're on the future site of the White Sheep Inn," she declared with pride.

Ana turned to her, excitement evident in her wide green eyes. "This is the land Yvonne bought up the hill years ago? All of this?" she asked as she made a sweeping movement with her arm.

"Yes, all of it," she replied with a chuckle.

"This is way more land than needed for the inn, though. Do you know what she had in mind?"

Melodie looked down at the white snow, so pure it sparkled with blue light. She wished she'd had more time to discuss the details of her grandmother's plans, but all she could do now was extrapolate the little she did know. "She had quite a vision. I'm pretty sure she had it all figured out, but unfortunately, I don't know everything she had in mind, no. She wanted to build flower gardens with pathways leading to benches and picnic tables where guests could appreciate the view and sunsets. She also talked about a large gazebo. She even mentioned doing weddings."

"Wow, I can't believe it. These are all wonderful ideas."

"She wanted to offer guests of the White Sheep Inn new ways to enjoy the sea. It was as if she'd read your article before you ever wrote it."

"The vision she had for this place is certainly in line with the ideas I wrote about in my article, but I have nothing to do with it. Your grandmother understood more about rising sea levels than we will ever know. Every time we talked about it when we walked together, I had the feeling she knew exactly what I was going to say before I said it. She knew what needed to be done, and obviously she was getting ready to do it."

"Yeah, well, she might have had time to do it before she passed away if I hadn't been holding her back with my stubbornness." She sighed with frustration and blinked several times to chase away her tears. She felt Ana's arms close around her and leaned her forehead against her shoulder, feeling protected from the cold as much as comforted from the regrets she hadn't openly disclosed until now.

"There's no point beating yourself up about that now," she whispered. "But you know what you have to do, right?"

She nodded against Ana's shoulder. She knew exactly what she had to do. She'd held her grandmother back, but the only way to make up for it was to bring her vision to life now. "I do. But I'm going to need your help to do it right. To make sure everything we do is best for the environment. To find as much financial help as we can. To make this place perfect. I want the White Sheep Inn to set an example for everyone else."

"That sounds exciting," she said with a light in her eyes, smiling with anticipation.

"So you'll help me?"

"Of course," she exclaimed before she hugged her. "We'll do this together for Yvonne."

"And for Thomas."

"And for Thomas."

They kissed and turned toward the sea to take in the view one more time before they walked back toward the street where they'd left the car.

"I was thinking we could even build a small home on the opposite side of the land, closer to the street. We wouldn't get the view but I'd be close to work."

"That sounds perfect."

"Even if my father stays with us?" she asked tentatively, afraid she might be asking too much. Although she wanted nothing more than to eventually share a home with Ana, she knew she couldn't turn her back on her father. She couldn't do it to him, to Thomas, or to herself.

"As long as he keeps teaching me how to fix things around the inn," she teased before she added more seriously, "I like your dad, you know that. And I think he likes me too. He did promise he'd forgive me as soon as you did."

"Oh, well, it's a done deal then." She chuckled as they got to the car and placed their snowshoes in the trunk. Then she opened the door on the passenger's side of the car for Ana. Instead of getting in, Ana grabbed her gloved hand and their eyes met.

"I don't know why you decided to forgive me, but I want you to know I don't take it for granted. I love you, Melodie. And I promise I will never leave again."

Hearing the words felt wonderful even though she already knew they were true. "I told you. I did it for me. Weren't you the one who told me that's how forgiveness works?" Ana smiled as she nodded. "And you can't leave even if you wanted to. We have too much to do."

They both turned to the marks left by their snowshoes on Yvonne's land, exchanging promising smiles and contemplating the work ahead of them.

EPILOGUE

Three and a half years later

"Kevin went inside to get the cake. Get ready to sing," Melodie announced as she snuck in behind Ana and wrapped her arms around her waist before kissing the back of her neck. Ana took one more deep breath of the wild roses they'd planted on the edge of the cliff, bordering that entire side of the property. It was a natural choice for the region and left a unique, strong perfume in the air. She took one last shot with her camera. "You do love your roses, don't you?"

"They're survivors. I respect that. They grow just about anywhere, and they love being by the sea almost as much as you do."

"Yeah, but like me, they seem to do fine on top of the hill too."

Ana turned and kissed Melodie on the lips. "Well we're all survivors, if you ask me. If we weren't we couldn't have made all of this happen." They both looked at the White Sheep Inn, firmly standing on its new foundations as if it had always been there. It had not been easy, but they'd finally received help from the city and provincial governments to make the move. They would have found a way to move the inn regardless, but Ana hoped their small victory would serve as a precedent for other home and business owners who would eventually decide to relocate. Two storms had hit the shores in the past three years, destroying more properties, and people were finally getting the message.

Once they'd successfully relocated the inn, they'd used the money from the sales of the duplex and Ana's house in Ithaca to build the small three-bedroom cottage that nested in the middle of mature trees at one corner of the property, almost invisible to the tourists who stayed at the inn. Finally, they'd built the gardens and the gazebo together, with Jerome's help. They'd decided to inaugurate the gazebo today by celebrating Thomas's fifth birthday. They were in the middle of the busy season and they'd invited all of their guests to the celebration, but Ana was grateful they'd all seemed to prefer getting busy with other activities. As a family, they didn't get to enjoy the gardens often, and today was a special occasion.

"Here he comes, let's go," Melodie prompted, interrupting her thoughts. They joined Thomas, Jerome and Nicole in the gazebo before Kevin arrived with the colorful sheet cake on which he'd lit five candles. The soccer-themed design created with icing on top of the cake seemed to have the effect they'd expected, judging by the excitement in Thomas's big blue eyes as he mouthed the word "Wow!"

As they sang "Happy Birthday" with enthusiasm, albeit completely off-key, Ana watched Miller lay on the cold concrete pavers under the table and she took a picture of him. He didn't enjoy the heat of the summer in his old days. Ana dreaded the day they'd lose his companionship. Not only would they lose the best canine companion any family could dream of, but it would also be like losing another part of Yvonne.

She turned to the wooden sign hanging at the entrance of the garden on which Melodie had used fancy lettering stencils to paint the words that reminded her Yvonne would always remain with them in some way: *"Les Jardins d'Yvonne."* Yvonne's Gardens.

Thomas made a wish and successfully blew out all five candles. "I want this soccer ball," he announced when Melodie started cutting the cake. Nicole helped by serving the portions of cake Melodie had placed in dessert plates. Their relationship improved each time Nicole visited, and they'd even developed a new, deep connection focused on Thomas. Ana doubted Melodie would ever call Nicole "Mom," but she knew better than anyone nothing was impossible.

She finished her piece of cake and left the empty dish on the table before she walked back to the edge of the cliff to take pictures of the sea, a favorite hobby of hers, although she often used some of her shots in the numerous articles she wrote about the relocation of the inn and other properties in Sainte-Luce-Sur-Mer.

Thomas quickly joined her. "Do you see white sheeps today?" he asked as he raised his arms for her to pick him up. He wasn't tall enough to see over the rosebushes and loved to hear her talk about the many different phenomena she observed on the Saint-Laurent.

She put her camera down to take him in her arms and pointed to the waves. "There are whole flocks of them today. Do you see all the white sheep running on water?"

"Yes. But they're not really sheeps, right?"

She chuckled, and not because he'd added an "s" to the word "sheep." She never corrected his pluralisation of the word because it made sense. There was more than one sheep, after all. She laughed because of the way he asked the same questions and made her repeat the same information over and over again. "You're right. They're not. But what are they then? Do you remember?"

"Uh…small waves?"

"Yes, they are. But what makes them white?"

"Oh, I know, I know. Foam," he answered with pride.

"That's right. You're so smart," Melodie said as she arrived behind them and tickled him. "They do look like sheep, though."

"No they don't," he yelled through laughter.

"Yes they do," she insisted. "Mammie Nicole is about to leave. Go say goodbye and then we'll go try out your present on the beach, okay?"

"Cool," he barely took the time to answer before he ran back to the gazebo. They'd given him a kite for his birthday and he was dying to see it fly.

"I'll get the towels for the cabins."

"They're already in the car," Melodie answered, waving her hand dismissively.

The towels were for the three tiny houses they'd installed on the beach where the inn used to stand. They were probably the part of their endeavor that brought her the most pride. Equipped with solar panels, small propane tanks, and compostable toilets, they were completely off the grid and appealed to eco-tourists so much that they were considering adding two more next year. More importantly, they were inspiring others to replace their permanent homes on the beach with sustainable, mobile structures similar to their tiny cabins. They were making progress, and every time she thought that progress wasn't coming fast enough, she heard Yvonne's voice in her mind. *Keep planting seeds.*

"I think the gazebo will be a huge success, don't you?" Melodie asked as she turned toward the large wooden structure.

"I do. Are you still thinking about using it and the gardens for weddings?"

"It was part of Mammie's plan, so yes, but I think we should wait until next year to get started. I still have a lot of research to do."

"Okay, that makes sense. But you know, what might help is if we tried it out first." As she reached into her pocket, her heart raced so fast she thought she might lose her nerve, but one look into Melodie's light blue, expectant eyes assured her she was making the right move. She took the simple white gold ring she'd chosen out of her pocket and held it in front of her, as if it could ask the question she hadn't voiced yet.

Somehow it worked, as Melodie quickly put the easy puzzle together, her eyes wide open and her smile stretching from ear to ear before she threw her arms around her neck and pulled her into a tight embrace. "Yes," she murmured.

"Yes?"

"Yes," she said louder as she pulled away and offered her finger on which Ana slipped the gold band. "When did you think of that?"

"A while ago. Don't you know I'm full of brilliant ideas?" Melodie kissed her softly but with clear intentions to take things further later.

"I do know. But usually it takes time for your ideas to grow on me. This one came out fully grown, like boom!"

"That's what you think, but you have no idea how long ago I planted that seed. No idea at all."

Bella Books, Inc.

Women. Books. Even Better Together.

P.O. Box 10543
Tallahassee, FL 32302

Phone: 800-729-4992
www.bellabooks.com

CPSIA information can be obtained
at www.ICGtesting.com
Printed in the USA
LVHW042013191218

601088LV00001B/41/P